The Tragic Fate of Matty Coyle

To order additional copies, please contact us.
BookSurge, LLC
www.booksurge.com
I-866-308-6235
orders@booksurge.com

The Tragic Fate of Matty Coyle

Malcolm Haslett

2006

The Tragic Fate of Matty Coyle

AUTHOR'S NOTE

All the characters in this book are entirely fictitious. Many of the place names refer to real locations in County Derry, but details of the topography may have been changed.

My sincere thanks go to Dr Neil Jarman of the Institute for Conflict Research in Belfast, and Dr Dominic Bryan of the Institute for Irish Studies at Queen's University, Belfast, for their kind permission to quote from their study "From Riots to Rights: Nationalist Parades in the North of Ireland" Coleraine,1998. ISBN I 85923 IIO 7.

Some non-Irish friends have said they find the political references a bit confusing, and have asked me to add a short explanation of the terminology. But I think it would probably be enough to say that the terms Nationalist, Republican and Catholic are generally associated with those in Northern Ireland who believe in a united Ireland; while Unionist, Loyalist, Orangeman and Protestant (or 'Prod') refer to those who want to keep a link with Great Britain.

I.

I've always had a thing about doors. They invite you through to see what's on the other side. If I hadn't gone through the door in my father's attic I wouldn't have found the notebooks. And then I would never have heard of Matty Coyle or of his cruel fate.

The door was hidden away in a corner, behind a chimney breast, and locked. There was no key to it that I could find. So I had a neighbour come and saw round the lock, and open the door to the tiny room beyond.

It was full of the sort of things you always find stuffed away in attics. Chests full of moth-eaten clothes. An old hat-stand with a compartment for umbrellas. Piles of old books (a twelve-volume History of the First World War among them). And a trunk full of legal papers.

And the notebooks.

Notebooks? They were just plain exercise books, from the school where my father had once taught. Filled during his later life with jottings, recollections of his childhood and youth. I took them to the desk in the old man's bedroom, at the back of the decaying old house. The window in front of me looked out over a lake surrounded by trees. It was just three days since we had laid him to rest over there, at the bottom of the graveyard, on a cold, windy day with the high elms tossing angrily above us. The relatives had all departed now, the ones I knew and the ones I had never known existed. It was painful to go through the empty house, among his belongings, but I knew that if I didn't do it now I probably never would.

Two of the exercise books, the ones with dull orange covers, were full. The neat, carefully formed words hung precariously on the printed blue lines, like so much fragile crockery perched on shelves. The third book, which had a mauve cover, had never been completed. It ended suddenly, half way through.

Stories. In the first book it was stories from his childhood. How he had fallen out of a tree and caught his eyebrow on the stump of a branch. I had heard that story before. 'Lucky I didn't lose an eye,' he had said more than once. 'If it had been just an inch lower...'

Stories of the troubles. 1916, 1917 and on up to 1921, 1922. How the bullets had whistled over the garden one sunny evening when he was playing there with his brothers, as the Sherwood Foresters battled the IRA for control of that corner of Derry.

Later, in the second book now, a lot of stories from his time as a student, travelling for the first time to Dublin, now the capital of the 'Free State'. And then back at holiday time to see his parents. How on one occasion, just before he left for the start of term, his mother had scolded him for some trivial matter, but had then appeared at the kitchen door as he left the yard and waved goodbye in a strange, almost timid way. Three days later, in Dublin, he heard the news of her sudden death.

Visits to the country, through all this time, to visit the farm in the Roe valley where his own father, my grandfather, had been brought up, one of eleven children...The third, unfinished notebook was almost entirely about these visits.

And it was here that I chanced on the name of Matty Coyle and began to wonder about my father's past.

My father would have been into his twenties by this time, evidently an open, gregarious man, popular among his peers. Especially popular with the country relatives who admired him so much for his education. For my father had not only been teaching for several years, in various places north and south of the border, but had travelled to England and even France, to learn the smattering of French with which he was to embarrass us for the rest of his life. To his country cousins, however, this seemed like the pinnacle of academic achievement, and my father was much admired by them. He was also, I think, genuinely liked.

I only briefly dipped into this third exercise book. By the time he wrote it, my father must have been suffering from the onset of the dementia which was to blight his final years. Sometimes he would have quite lucid spells, when he was almost normal. But then, increasingly, his mind would just go blank. He wouldn't even recognise us some of the time. And in the third notebook the old man's writing had become more spidery, the words less confident, the memories confused and befuddled. Some of the stories he began to relate would take off boldly, then end in mid-air, in mid-sentence. The narrative would begin again, often on a tack which it was difficult to relate to the part that went before, and sometimes it would start on what seemed to be an altogether different train of thought, spurred by goodness knows what subconscious associations hidden deep in the crevices of the ageing man's consciousness.

I had begun to lose interest in this rambling hodgepodge of barely comprehensible memories, and was about to put the exercise books back in the box where I had found them, when my eye fell on a sentence on the very last page. I lost it for a moment, and had to search through the lines of wandering scrawl for several minutes. Yes, there it was, a sentence written with a firmer hand, by itself up near the top of the page.

"*Did you forgive Matty Coyle, Old Bob asked me, before you took him off into the glen that last night?*"

I looked at the sentence again. What on earth did it mean? What sort of 'last journey' did it refer to?

I read on, right to the end of the next paragraph, which was also the very end of my father's narrative. But there was no further mention of anyone called Matty Coyle. So I glanced back through the pages that had come before.

My father had evidently been visiting the farm at Banagher where his father, my grandfather, and many generations before that, had been raised…

In my childhood it had seemed an unreal place, full of excitable hens and complaining ducks, and looming, menacing dark monsters which I later discovered were called cows. And the inhabitants were uncles and aunts and cousins with strange names, like Willie John and Robert James and Mary Anne, some of them as fierce and disturbing as the animals, others warm and welcoming and fussing over the welfare of the visitors from the town.

On the occasion my father was referring to on the last page of his diary he had fallen out with Uncle Robert James, or Old Bob, as the family called him. The subject, I guessed, was politics.

"Uncle Bob turned on me," my father wrote, *"and told me I could go back to the city at once if that was my attitude. 'Down here,' he said hotly, 'we can't afford to show this 'forgiveness' of enemies that you talk about. 'If we did,' he said, 'you just watch them. They'll have us off our land in no time at all.' I said something about the church which he, more than anyone in the family, attended so regularly, and the teaching on forgiveness which he must have heard there over and over again. He gave me such a look of thunder, the angriest look I had ever seen, and he said nothing for several moments. Then he said: 'Aye, Christian forgiveness. You and your friends, Lexie, would know all about that, the way you dealt with Matty Coyle. Don't think we didn't know about what happened that night.'*

'Did you forgive Matty Coyle, Old Bob asked me, before you took him off into the glen that last night?'"

Several lines below this was another sentence, almost illegible because the writing had become an agitated scrawl.

"I've never answered that question. They were always on my back. I should have told them all. Long ago. The truth."

I stopped reading and went back over the passage I had just read, astonished. What was it all about? I rapidly skimmed again through the last few pages of my father's disjointed narrative. But the only references to Matty Coyle were these, right near the end, referring to a 'last journey'.

Had my father, as he wrote, been preparing—nervously, tentatively—to make some admission, some confession that he never had time to complete? Had he wanted to talk to somebody about an incident which lay on his conscience, and had lain there for most of his life? Whichever way I looked at it, that seemed the only explanation.

But what did he have to confess? Who was this Matty Coyle, and what had become of him?

I put the exercise book aside, thinking to examine it and the other two for further clues at some future date.

*****

That evening I sat with my brother in the darkened sitting room of the empty house. The silence was broken only by the relentless ticking of the enormous grandfather clock in the hall. It seemed to echo round the house, reminding us of times past and the people who would never hear it again.

"The name Matty Coyle, does it mean anything to you?" I asked.

He looked at me sharply, and for a moment I thought my brother knew something I didn't. But the moment passed, and he said only: "Can't say that it does...Should it? Was he a friend of the old man?"

I shook my head. "Don't know. It's just that there's a reference to someone called that in one of those old exercise books where he jotted down his 'memoirs'."

"Ah yes...'Searching for Time Lost somewhere in County Derry'...I think maybe we had relations who were called Coyle, somewhere on his mother's side."

"Oh?" I said, surprised. "It's not a name I've ever heard mentioned."

"No, bit of a dark secret, I think..."

"Really? Why was that?"

He paused for a moment.

"Well, you see, I think they were Catholics."

2.

On the plane back to London I thought of something else, a memory of my own which just might have had a connection with Matty Coyle.

It must have been twenty years earlier, or more. I had been home from England, staying in my father's big, dark house, where he had lived alone since mother died. The only other person there was 'Granny', my mother's mother. She had never hit it off with her son-in-law, but he, out of a sense of duty, I suppose, or maybe a false sense of guilt at my mother's early death, had agreed to take the old lady in, since none of her other children wanted her. My grandmother could be very tiresome indeed, with her dogmatic political views and her constant gripes and moans about everything around her. She and my father quarrelled endlessly. But she was old and frail and unwanted, and in secret he obviously felt sorry for her. And so did I. I even allowed her to exploit me, by agreeing to run errands for her. These were mostly in the direction of the nearest off-licence, to keep her supplied with the half bottles of brandy which were her only solace in bitter old age.

One day, when I was alone with her after one of my errands, she said something very strange. Of course by that time almost everything she said was strange, in the sense that it was mixed up and nonsensical. (Only a few months later, indeed, she drank a little bit too much of her brandy, keeled over and hit her head on the dresser, and never recovered.) But for a couple of years before that she had been taking on board some very odd ideas indeed. One of her favourite obsessions, and she really seemed to believe it, was that the British government had been taken over by Joseph Stalin. From his grave, no doubt. She was convinced that from now on anyone who said anything out of turn was more or less certain to end up in the salt mines. She had also persuaded herself that she, Ivy Walters, was a prime target for this sort of persecution. "If they come to the door, Adrian," she would whisper to me conspiratorially, "whatever you do, don't let them in! Say that I've gone to South Africa, or maybe South America."

And the mention of South America would set her off on one of her lengthy, endlessly repeated, stories…This one was about the time she crossed the ocean to Chile to see her son, my uncle, who was working there as a teacher. In mid-Atlantic, she would tell us, there had been a terrible storm, and the waves rose so high that on her way to dinner she was hurled from one side of the dining room to the other. But she had never been sea-sick, she maintained. No, not even though the sea became so rough at one point that the water all poured out of her bath, and her still sitting in it!

Just this once, however, she told a very different story, one I hadn't heard before. We were sitting in the conservatory at the back of the house, with a pale June sun trying to break through the perennial cloud. I was aware that she had been giving me sidelong glances for some time, as if debating whether to tell me something. Something, perhaps, that she wasn't supposed to.

"Such a pity," she said suddenly, apropos of nothing in particular, "about that poor young man. Didn't have a chance. And they tried to keep it quiet for years. I doubt if anyone has told the full truth, even today..."

She gave me another surreptitious look, to see what effect her words were having on me.

"What young man was that?" I asked innocently. "Anyone I should know?"

"No, no," she gave a sinister little chuckle. "It was long before you were born...They found him in that dreadful place...in all that water and mud. Near that awful farm your father took me to once...Hmph, didn't stay there long. Not what I was used to. They had to take me to a hotel, quite some distance away, near the sea, I remember. But I wasn't sorry to get away from all that mud and stench...and the next day I took the train back to Dublin."

"But what happened to this young man you mentioned?" I persisted.

Her face went suddenly blank and she stared at me in incomprehension. "What did you say?" she said.

"You were mentioning a young man, and something terrible that had happened to him."

She continued to look at me in puzzlement.

"Something happened to him, something to do with mud and water."

"Oh, that one! Yes, he came to a bad end. Terrible it was...Still, he probably deserved it. There's no smoke without fire, is what I say! He probably did something to deserve it..."

"To deserve what?"

She looked at me again, this time with suspicion written all over her face.

"But they killed him, of course. Don't you remember that? You were there at the time, weren't..."

Suddenly she realised she had confused me with my father, and in an instant she became flustered and edgy. Clearly she had said more than she had intended, and much more than she was supposed to.

"I don't know any more," she muttered. "That's all they told me. Ask your father if you want to know more..."

But for some reason I never did. Perhaps I thought the story was just another of Granny's wild imaginings. Perhaps I sensed that my father wouldn't tell me anything, even if there was something in the fragmented story the old woman had told. Perhaps I just forgot.

But now, high above the clouds over the Irish Sea, that conversation came back to me. And as we passed over Liverpool I bent down and opened my brief-case, and took out the mauve exercise book to read it one more time.

3.

"You haven't heard a word I've said," Steve said wearily across the desk.

I turned away from the window and the depressing sight of the rain splattering down on the car park outside.

"Uh, no. Sorry. What did you say?"

"We really do have to get this Havering market project under way. The borough architect is coming tomorrow and we don't even know which site has been approved. You've got to chase it up, Adrian!"

"Yeah…Yes. I'll phone Williams right away…"

He looked at me curiously. "Anything the matter?" he asked.

"No…Nothing. Just something on my mind. About my father's will…"

"Ah, I see," he said, trying to sound sympathetic. He knew I'd 'gone a bit funny' about my father's death. That's what I'd heard him say to one of the office staff the day before.

"Look," I told him, making a sudden decision, "you're not going to thank me for this, Steve, but I really have to go back to Ireland soon. When we've got this market thing off the ground, I'll have to leave you to handle it for a while…"

I could feel his sympathy fast evaporating.

"What's the problem?" he said, tight-lipped.

"Something I found in my father's will," I said vaguely. "Probably nothing, but I don't want to take any chances."

"Anything I can help with?" he asked. "I once worked in a solicitor's office, you know."

Blast, I'd forgotten that.

"No…thanks anyway. My brother wasn't very clear about it on the phone. But he was obviously worried."

"Yeah, these probate things can be quite complicated, I know…Well, if you have to go, you have to go."

Driving home I wondered if I wasn't making too much of the whole thing. But the truth was that I had been more deeply upset by my father's death than I at first realised. I kept having dizzy spells in the office, and found that my mind often just went blank as I sat there trying to write reports for the council officers. I didn't know whether this was normal, the result of the stress of bereavement, or whether there was more to it than that. There was no reason to connect it with the curious passage I had found in the exercise book. And yet the phrase 'did you forgive him?' kept running through my mind, no matter how often I tried to blot it out of my thoughts. Obviously it was bugging me at some level of my consciousness that I hadn't even realised existed. I hadn't been sleeping well either since I got back to London, and I kept dreaming weird dreams about lynchings in the Deep South and witches being burned in Cornwall or New England. Several times I'd woken in the middle of the night in a cold sweat, with the feeling I had to do something urgently, something which would have a profound effect on my life and the lives of people around me.

Yet I had only the haziest idea why I felt like this, or what it was I thought I had to do.

There was little doubt in my mind, however, that it was connected in some way to the still shadowy figure of someone called Matty Coyle. A person who had once known my father. And had gone with him on a final journey.

4.

The newspaper office looked out over the river, with its tidy embankment lined with lime trees. This was a plantation town if ever there was one, trim and businesslike. And still, to a certain degree, self-confident, even if some of the old certainties had been blown away with the troubles.

The office was bright and neat, its occupant polite but distant. He had heavy-rimmed glasses and a high dome of a head. What was left of his hair was dark, and neatly combed. On the table in front of him lay the name-tab **D.P. Beckton.**

"You can just check on our website, you know...It has an archive, and all you have to do..."

"But your website only covers the last few years. I wanted to look at editions back in the 1930s. 1935 or 1936."

He seemed taken aback. "We don't have records any more for that period," he said. "1935 did you say? No, most of the pre-war archives were got rid of long ago...We just didn't have the space."

"You kept nothing? Nothing at all?"

He shook his balding head. "I personally supervised the clear-out when I took over the 'Constitution' five years ago. It was just cluttering up rooms we needed for our new features office..."

There was an uneasy silence.

"You may find there's a full set of back copies in the British Library, in the newspaper archives at Colindale...That's in north-west London," he added helpfully.

"I know," I said. "I live and work in London."

"Ah, so it will be easy for you to find what you want there..."

There was something I found irritating about this man, with his bald head and self-confident eyes staring fixedly at me through unnaturally thick lenses. And I was having trouble working out his accent. At first it had seemed local, educated but definitely Ulster. Now I was beginning to pick up a definite trans-Atlantic twang.

"I've just come over from London," I said drily. "I wasn't expecting a newspaper to have destroyed all its old issues."

He lifted his shoulders in a gesture of helplessness.

"Guess you'll just have to go home again...You say you wanted to research your family's background. Can I ask what specifically it was you were interested in?"

I didn't feel much like telling him. "Oh, it's something from way back…"

"Yes, 1935 ," he said. "But what was it?"

I looked at him coolly. "I'm sure it's not anything that would ring a bell with…anyone of our generation. Especially someone who, forgive me, seems to have a trans-Atlantic background. Or am I wrong?"

He raised his eyebrows, genuinely surprised. "What, me? You think that… I'm American?"

"One or two hints in your voice would suggest you've spent some time there."

He threw back his head and laughed.

"Well, I did spend a few months there once…in my twenties. But you're wrong. I'm County Derry, born and bred."

"Your name…Beckton. Is that a County Derry name?"

"Not particularly," he said, suddenly shifting forward in his chair and tapping the desk with a pencil he'd been twirling in his fingers. "I think in our case it was once Huguenot. Beccatin, or something like that…But you haven't told me what it is you were looking for in the back copies…"

"As I say, I don't expect it's anything you, or anyone else, would remember."

"Try me," he insisted, and his jaw set in a strangely challenging smile.

I hesitated for a moment, then said:

"I wanted to look up an incident involving a certain Matty Coyle…"

He was still looking at me with his oddly humourless smile.

"This incident took place in Coleraine?"

"No, in another part of County Derry, not far from Dungiven."

"What sort of incident was this?"

"I think…he may have been killed."

Again he raised his eyebrows. It seemed to be an annoying habit of his.

"Killed? You mean murdered?"

"Yes, I think so."

"You think so? But you don't know for sure…"

"No, that's why I wanted to check for details of the incident."

He looked at me searchingly. "What details do you have?"

"None."

"None? Then how do you know that this…what did you call him? Matty Conlon?"

"Matty Coyle."

"How do you know that he was murdered?"

I decided that Mr Beckton was asking too many questions. "I'd prefer to keep that to myself," I said stiffly.

The editor of the Constitution pulled a face.

"Don't want to reveal your sources, is that it?" he said, with more than a hint of mockery.

"Let's say my source is a private letter. Written by someone who's no longer alive."

He sat there studying me with his owlish eyes. I had the impression he was contemplating how he could winkle more out of me on the subject of my search.

"A letter written by a relative of yours?" he asked.

He caught me off guard and my surprise betrayed to him the accuracy of his guess. But all I said was:

"Maybe."

He grimaced. But then he merely shrugged and said:

"Leave your address and phone number with me, Mr McCausland, and if I find out anything I'll be in touch...Now, if you don't mind, I'm quite a busy man. Have to put a newspaper to bed, even if it is only a weekly...As I say, you should look in the archives at Colindale...Miss McFarlane will show you out," he said, and gave me another of his humourless smiles.

Reluctantly, I got up to go. This man, I felt sure, knew more than he was willing to admit.

5.

"They've all gone to Bovevagh," said Michael, when the dogs had finally ceased their barking. "It's the first anniversary of Old Bob's death. He was over there visiting his only remaining sister when he passed away...That was on his birthday, his 99th. Today would have been his hundredth!"

Michael was the only person left on the farm. I had swung the car into the bare concrete expanse of the yard and he emerged alone from the 'new house', the modern two-storeyed residence that now stood on the side overlooking the 'glen'. The old house, the long, thatched building across the yard where we had been entertained in the old days was now a home for only chickens and pigs.

"Will they be back tonight, Michael?" I asked.

"Aye, they'll be home by the evening, they said. Leaving me in charge for the day is OK. But they wouldn't want me to take over their farm for more than that!"

I laughed. Michael was a Catholic, and we both knew what he meant. I had always liked him. He was about sixty himself and had worked as a labourer for the family all his life. Why he had chosen our family in particular I could never quite understand, since there were plenty of prosperous Catholic farmers he could have worked for. Once he had told me it had something to do with my own father. He was "a great fellow", Michael had said. That had cheered me, though I had never been quite sure how seriously to take him.

For some forty years now, for six days a week, Michael had walked over to the farm at the crack of day from his cottage on the other side of Banagher glen, just "under the mountain" as he liked to describe it. He was an affable, unflappable man of below medium height with mild, wrinkled features and hair which had seemed to be grey ever since I had met him, twenty or thirty years before. He appeared to hold no grudges against anyone, and as a result was himself liked by all. How he had managed to avoid an argument with my relatives over all those years was nothing short of a miracle, given the strong feelings of some family members when it came to politics or religion. If the conversation took a turn in that direction Michael would simply sit there and pass a few non-committal phrases, or make a joke, or simply remain silent. Rarely did he enter into detailed discussion.

"They'll probably be back around six or seven...But come in and have a cup of something. It's a wee while since we saw you down here, young Adrian."

The wee while must have been ten years or more, I thought.

When we were installed at the kitchen table with mugs of thick, sugary tea, he asked me what had brought me over after so long. Then he broke off.

"I was forgetting," he said after a moment's pause, "your father died a few weeks back, didn't he? I was sorry to hear that. I liked him the best of your family. He was always...a fair-minded man."

I looked over the table at him, wondering why he had said that in particular. But it brought me some reassurance. If there had been some sinister mystery in my father's past life, surely someone like Michael would have known about it.

"Michael," I said, "does the name Matty Coyle mean anything to you?"

His reaction surprised me. There was no dramatic gesture, no exclamation or even a suspicious narrowing of the eyes. Michael just said nothing. And went on saying nothing, holding his mug in his hands and staring out over the tree-filled glen at the back of the house. After a minute or so I felt I had better prompt him.

"Michael, you don't have to tell me anything you don't want. But the name has come up...recently, and there seems to be some mystery attached to it. I wondered if you knew what it was."

He turned his gaze back towards me and I saw there a coolness which I had never associated with Michael before.

"You'd be best just to forget that name, I think, Mr Adrian," he said. It didn't seem that he was angry so much as troubled.

"So you do know something about Matty Coyle?"

Michael shook his head.

"Some things are best left unmentioned," he said. "It all happened when I was a very small boy, so I couldn't really tell you what happened myself. You see, they never told me. Nobody ever talked about it, either your people or mine..."

He meant the families, no doubt.

"But who was he, Michael? You can at least tell me that..."

Michael got up and went to the kitchen range to pour himself another cup of tea. He was so engrossed in his thoughts that he forgot to offer me one.

"He was a youngish man, I believe," he said, "about your father's age. And he was a teacher, in Ballymully, I think...And apart from that all I know is that he died...He was drowned, in the mill pond down in the glen there." He nodded in the direction of the tree-filled valley that snaked its way past the back of the house.

I put down my mug. I have to confess I was shaken.

For at least two reasons. Firstly, my fears of some dark secret involving my father and Matty Coyle had been confirmed. And secondly, because of where it had happened...

Banagher Glen cut its way through the pleasant, rolling farmland of central Derry like a woolly green serpent until it opened out a mile or two below the

THE TRAGIC FATE OF MATTY COYLE

farm into the broad valley of the Roe. It had always been a playground for me, a place where my brother and I had roamed in the carefree days of our visits to the farm. It had never been associated in my mind with darkness or death, or anything sinister. For us it had been a land of hidden wonders.

The mill lake that Michael referred to was maybe half a mile below the farm, a calm, slightly mysterious expanse of water over which the trees, to my childish way of thinking, had always seemed to bend their heads in awe and reverence. And below the lake there was the mill itself. What it had been used for, flax or grain or something else, I had never bothered to ask. But to my youthful mind it was a place of adventure and romance, complete with a real water wheel of rusty iron which had of course long since ceased to turn, though the mill race which once had driven it continued to flow out of the lake.

"He drowned?" I asked, dumbfounded. "Was it an accident? Or was... somebody responsible?"

"That's exactly what nobody would ever tell me. My family would never talk about it. I gathered from the things some people said that everyone thought it was not an accident. And from the way they spoke about it I had the impression they had their suspicions about who it was that did it..."

"And who was that, Michael?"

Michael was beginning to look very uncomfortable. He began to swill the tea round in the bottom of his mug and kept looking out the window over to the far side of the glen.

"You'll understand, Master Adrian, that these things were just gossip... And later I was to hear other versions..."

"But what was the version you heard in your family?"

"That it was people from your side of the glen...I mean from your family and their friends...who did it."

I let the words sink in, and then nodded.

"But that didn't prevent you from coming later, from coming over and working for them, for the McCauslands?"

He shook his head and smiled. "I've always had good relations with your family, Mr Adrian. No reason to complain about them. Very forthright people, sometimes. Express their views very readily. But honest people, as good as you'll find in these parts."

I paused.

"So does that mean you didn't really believe the stories, that my family were among the people who...killed Matty Coyle?"

Michael shook his head again. Now that the subject had been broached he seemed readier to talk. "For a start, nobody ever knew for certain that he was killed. No one was ever convicted, if you see what I mean. It was only what people supposed...What's more, it always struck me..." He hesitated, as if not quite sure how to express what he was going to say. "It always struck me that some people were too certain that it was a killing."

I looked at him. "You mean, somebody was trying to…to make a bit of propaganda out of it?"

He nodded, pensively. "Could be. Could be…"

"And you said earlier you'd heard other versions…"

"Yes…" his voice trailed away, and for a while he seemed to be wondering how to pick up the threads of the story. Finally he broke into a chuckle.

"The Prods, of course, said it was us Catholics who done it!"

I smiled too. "The usual story," I said. "Each side blaming the other…"

His smile faded. "But the trouble is, that story wasn't altogether daft…I heard later that Matty had enemies on the Catholic side too. You see, it seems that our Matty was a complicated character…"

"Complicated? In what way was he complicated, Michael?"

Michael took a deep breath.

"Well, for a start…his father was Catholic and his mother Protestant. He was from a mixed family…"

I nodded. "My brother Eric says he thinks Matty might have been related to us."

"I don't know about that, Mr Adrian, but I suppose it's not impossible… What I do know is that Matty Coyle was friends with your father."

"With my father? Are you sure about that?"

"Pretty sure. Your father was a lot older than me. He was already grown up when I first remember him. He was a teacher too, but somewhere a long way away. I think he'd already gone to Enniskillen by then. But he used to come here on visits. And I remember one evening, round the dinner table in the old house…this would have been years after Matty Coyle died, probably around the time I first met him, when I had just started working here. And someone mentioned Matty's name…"

Michael stopped, as if trying to remember the details.

"And what happened then?" I asked impatiently. "How did the others react?"

"I'm trying to remember, Mr Adrian…I can't be certain, but I think the name just slipped out by chance. It was your cousin James, maybe, who mentioned it. And all the others were silent, and looked at your father. And then Maud, Old Bob's wife, said to your father: 'You liked him well, didn't you, Lexie?' Or something like that. Yes, it was definitely something like that…"

"But you didn't pick up any more details, Michael, about what happened to Matty?"

"No, when I asked who Matty was they all looked at me as if I was the world's worst sinner…which of course I was, because I was the only Catholic there."

I smiled.

"And you don't remember anything else about Matty?"

"No…as I say, he was a teacher, like your father. But in a Catholic school, of course. And I think he had a sister, Her name was Laurie, or Lottie, or something. But if anything, people talked about her even less than they talked about Matty."

"They lived near here?"

"They lived with their mother, who was a cripple it seems, near Upperfields, on the other side of the glen. Near where I still live."

"But you never met any of them yourself, Michael?"

He shook his head. "They were all long gone by the time I remember," he said.

The turf shifted in the grate.

"Why was it you wanted to know, Mr Adrian?" Michael asked. "Why are you interested in Matty after all these years?"

"Oh, something I found among my fathers papers," I answered vaguely. "Something that set me wondering."

"Well I'm sorry I haven't been of much help."

"On the contrary, Michael, you've been of great help."

He had at least assured me that my father was not Matty Coyle's enemy, and would have had no reason to do him harm. Or so I thought.

6.

Michael told me he had chores to do. So I said that if he had no objection I would wander down into the glen and reacquaint myself with the spots I had known as a child.

He gave me a strange, half ironic look.

"You're not afraid of ghosts, then?"

I smiled at his attempt at humour.

"We all have to live with ghosts in this country, Michael," I said.

I found the narrow path leading down into the glen with some difficulty. The summer was now past, but it had been hot and humid. No one could remember weather like it, Michael had said. It had been as if there was always a thunder storm in the air. And the heat and damp had made the grass grow and the brambles spread, so that the top of the path was hard to locate. But at last I found it behind an enormous bramble bush, and decided it was just about passable, at the cost of a few tears in my sleeves and trousers.

Before I plunged down into the trees, however, I paused to view the broad sweep of countryside around.

To the west, beyond the glen, rose the smooth contours of the high country that divided the Roe valley from Derry and the wide basin of the Foyle. To my left, towards the south, was the long line of the Sperrins, their mellow contours a pale blue, and shimmering in the haze. I turned, and there behind me, to the east, were more hills, the fine range of crests that stretches up from the Glenshane pass in the south to the cliffs of Binevenagh in the north, dominated by the majestic shape of Benbradagh. Here every detail, every hedgerow or wall or white cottage, could be seen clearly. From various points along the ridge where they were burning the bracken or heather rose V-shaped blue-grey plumes of smoke, trailing away over the summits into the broad valley of the Bann beyond.

And at my feet lay the tree-filled glen itself, a band of deep green winding its way through the lighter patchwork of the farmland. This glen had always divided the McCausland farm from the poorer country beyond. It held in its leafy shade, I now knew, the key to murky secrets I had never even suspected. And yet as I gazed at it on that day it seemed greener, more peaceful and more beautiful than I had ever remembered it. Funny, I thought, it should be the other way round. Our memories are supposed to be richer and more idyllic than reality. But on that particular day, with its bright sunshine and gentle westerly breeze, the vivid emerald of the gently stirring treetops was almost mesmerising.

I began clambering down the steep track that plunged into the trees. It seemed to be much less used now than in the days of my youth. I had to explore several barely visible openings through the thorn bushes before I found one that yielded access to the moist shelter of the larger trees. Even under the roof of leaves it was hot and humid. The acrid stench of cow dung hung heavily on the air. Large bluebottles droned lazily past my ears, and there was a constant buzz of lighter insects all the way down through the undergrowth.

I was quite suddenly overcome by a sense of foreboding. Did I want to go any further? There was an oppressive silence in the wood, as if someone or something was waiting there for me. Was it wise to continue?

But the moment passed. What are you afraid of, I asked myself. There are no ghosts or hobgoblins here. Only trees. And memories.

Towards the bottom the trees thinned out a little and there was more space to observe and to breathe. The faint, rarely used track that led along the bottom of the glen wound in and out of the trees like some path in a fairy-tale leading to a robber's den or giant's castle. Not far away, a ceaseless gurgle from the middle of a thick band of bulrushes betrayed the presence of Banagher Burn, the brook which flowed through the glen and fed the lake further down the valley.

I turned right and wandered lazily along the track. It was calm here, and peaceful, and the flies and stench were no longer so oppressive. Within a couple of minutes I caught the gleam of water through the trees.

Again I stopped. What had Michael said? Matty Coyle had been drowned here, in the mill lake. Once more a voice inside my head told me to hold back, not to go any further.

But again I dismissed it as childish nonsense. It was just a lake, a stretch of water between wooded banks. I walked on.

The lake was much as I'd remembered it, long and narrow, no more than a hundred yards wide at its broadest point. I continued along its banks, gazing through the trunks of the waterside trees out over its still, flat surface. On that warm and sultry day the water lay like a sheet of glass, vividly reflecting the rich greenery of the beaches and oaks covering the opposite bank. The noise of the insects had returned, and seemed to intensify in the warm air that hung over the lake. Now and then a dragonfly would dart past, followed by the heavy drone of a bee or bluebottle.

The sun had now reached its midday zenith and I was beginning to feel the heat, so I stopped and took out my handkerchief to mop the beads of perspiration from my forehead. It was then that I noticed the small island near the far bank. It was little more than a mud bank really, though a number of stunted trees had taken root there amid a patch of sedge. I had forgotten about its existence. But now I recalled how, in my youth, I had secretly imagined making a raft from the branches of fallen trees and rowing out to the island, to take possession of it as my very own…

Once, I remembered, when the level of the lake had sunk so low that the tiny island was separated from the shore by no more than a narrow stretch of sickly grey mud, I had even attempted to reach it on foot. I'd seriously miscalculated, however, how treacherous the slimy mass surrounding the islet would be. After twenty yards I found my wellington boots were sinking deep into the ooze, until finally, when it began to rise within a few inches of the left boot's rim, I decided it was time to turn back. Too late! Both feet were now firmly embedded in the soft, clawing mud

In sudden panic I had thrown myself backwards, flat on the surface of the mud. Desperately I tried to crawl over it towards the bank. But my elbows now began to sink into the morass, and for one horrible moment my chin embedded itself in the grey slime. I pushed my face free and kicking my feet free from the boots, began to ease myself slowly back towards firmer land.

When I reached the bank I looked back. The boots, a fine new pair which had belonged to one of my cousins, had disappeared.

Sitting on the bank, wheezing madly as a result of my exertions, it had suddenly dawned on me just how close I had been to disaster. The later rebukes of my cousin and his mother, I found, were a small price to pay for my deliverance from the mud.

…I found that the memory had changed my mood completely. My mind was suddenly full of visions of dark figures extricating a man's body from the same clinging morass where I had so nearly perished. I tried to remember Michael's exact words. Had he said that Matty Coyle's body had been discovered somewhere near the island? I couldn't remember. But suddenly the stillness, the heaviness of the air, the drone of the insects, all seemed to speak of the presence of evil, an evil which, in my youth, I had never for a moment sensed.

I hurried on, anxious to see all that there was to see and then leave the wooded valley as soon as possible. I would go to the mill, where there was a road up out of the glen, and then proceed home by the country lanes which skirted it.

I followed the lake round the bend towards the place where, I knew, it ended in the low earth dam. To one side there would be the small stone bridge, and under it the swift-flowing mill race descending towards the great iron wheel by the mill house. Soon, through the foliage, I saw the grey stonework of the building. And as I emerged from the trees and came within view of the building I saw to my surprise that someone was already there.

7.

The mill stood on a spit of land between the mill race and the lake. It had been all spruced up. The overgrown lane which used to lead down to it from the other side of the glen had been cleared and tarred, and from a sign hanging over the tiny car park I learned that the mill was now a tea house. Open from ten a.m. to five, it said.

A family group had just finished their tea and scones and were getting into a car to drive off, leaving only one person sitting amid the wooden tables in the grassy enclosure beside the mill. As I approached I was able to observe him more closely. He was a lanky individual with wavy, light ginger hair very much thinning at the front. His gangling legs were stretched out before him as he studied some sort of document through rimless spectacles. He wore a blue checked shirt and jeans, and a pair of heavy but expensive boots. I nodded a greeting to him as I passed, and he grunted something back in a distracted sort of way.

I went into the little shop and gave my order, then went to sit outside. The best view of the lake was from the two tables on the parapet overlooking the water, one of which was already occupied by the man in glasses. I sat down at the other one. He looked up from his reading, which I noticed was not a book at all, but a map folded roughly into a rectangle.

"Nice weather," he said cheerfully, in what didn't seem quite a local accent.

"Yes, a bit too warm for me," I replied, swatting a fly away from my face.

He chuckled and went back to studying his map. A couple of minutes later, however, he looked up and asked:

"You from these parts?" The accent, I could now hear, was definitely not local. My new acquaintance had crossed the ocean to be here.

I nodded in reply. "Family farm is just up there, along the edge of the glen," I said, "though I've lived in London myself for a number of years."

"So you'll know a bit about the local history?" he asked.

My tea and scones had just arrived. "What sort of local history are you interested in?"

He pulled in a deep breath and gazed out over the tree-lined lake.

"I'm researching a book about industrial unrest between the wars."

"Here in County Derry?" I asked, a bit surprised.

"In the North as a whole."

I bit into the first scone. "Then what you're researching," I suggested, glancing over at him, "includes sectarian unrest."

I found he was looking straight at me, in a thoughtful way, as if wondering where the conversation was going to lead. Finally he said with a sigh: "You're certainly right there. What brings me to these parts is the affair of Brannigan's mill. That mean anything to you?"

I thought I had heard something, a long time in the past, about some sort of factory, a shirt factory I thought it was, which had been the focus of controversy in the early years of the Northern Irish state. But I had never known the details.

"That was somewhere close to Derry City, wasn't it?"

"No, no, it was here. Just down the road. If you're from these parts I'm surprised you didn't know that. The site of the mill was to have been at Upperfields, hardly a mile from here."

I was genuinely surprised, and said so.

"Of course they never completed it," my new acquaintance commented. "The Unionist government saw to that."

Again I expressed disbelief.

"Oh, it was a 'cause celebre'," he said, setting aside his map. "You see, Brannigan was an Irish American who had roots in this area. And he said he wanted to build a factory for the Catholics, to offset the discrimination they were suffering, especially at that time. It was the middle of the depression, you see. But of course there were loud protests from all the Unionists in the country, accusations that it was an attempt to 'import' Catholics into a Protestant area...though in fact it was in reality a very mixed area, and Upperfields itself was predominantly Catholic."

I had heard differently, but I didn't want to argue.

"So what happened? What caused the trouble?"

"After the work began there were a lot of 'accidents' began to happen at the work site. Builder's huts would be burned down and machinery would disappear, and that sort of thing. And the local Orangemen and the likes organised sort of vigilante gangs that drove round the country blaring their horns and trying to put the fear of death into the local Catholics...By the way, are you...?"

"No, I'm not a Catholic...But I'm interested in what you're saying. I didn't know much about it before."

"You should go and read about it in the archives of the local papers...the two Derry papers and maybe the Constitution in Coleraine..."

"Ha!" I laughed. "Not much point in going there. They've got rid of all their archives for that period. I tried to look something up myself last week, but they said the only copy I would find was on fiche in the British Library in London."

He looked at me oddly.

"That's strange," he said. "They opened up all the archives to me…"

"When?"

"Just two days ago."

I paused with a scone half way to my mouth.

"Was it Mr Beckton you spoke to, the editor?"

"Mr Darius Beckton. The very same. Seemed very ready to help me…"

I was flabbergasted, and sat there for a few moments trying to take this revelation in.

"Can I enquire what it was you were researching?" he asked quietly. "Could it have been something more sensitive than my request?"

"More sensitive than sectarian strife?" I laughed ironically. "Hardly. It was just some background about a man who was related to me, who lived…and died, in that same period actually. You see, my father died recently…"

"I'm sorry…"

"Don't worry…My father died, and that got me thinking about family history and all that sort of thing."

"Mmm." The sandy-haired man had suddenly gone thoughtful. For a while he let me eat my scones and down my tea. Then he said:

"My family were from round here too. They lived somewhere on the other side of the glen from your people's house. Somewhere up the side of the mountain. But when I went there with some of my remaining relatives we just couldn't find the place. It's been a ruin for years, they say…"

I laughed. "I know the feeling. When my father's Canadian cousin came over looking for the family homestead, my father told her it had been a ruin for years. But she insisted. So he crawled through the local lanes in the car, asking the local yokels if they knew where Moss's old house had once been. One of them told him there was nothing left of it, just a 'wheen o' stanes'…The Canadian cousin, of course, hadn't a clue what the man was talking about…"

"Excuse me, is that some sort of local dialect?"

"Yes, it's Ulster Scots for 'pile of stones'…Why?"

He was looking at me with a very earnest look. "Yes, you are a Protestant, aren't you?"

"What do you mean?"

"To make such a thing of the Scottish connection…"

I was taken aback. "It was only a story," I said innocently. "Something that just came into my mind…"

He smiled, but there was a slight chill in the air that hadn't been there before.

"By the way," I said, in an attempt to dispel it, "we haven't introduced ourselves. My name's Adrian, Adrian McCausland."

"Ray, Ray Conlon," he answered, accepting the handshake I offered. "But my mother's name was Brannigan."

"You mean, as in…"

"Yes," he said, "Old Al, as we called him, otherwise known as Aloysius Brannigan of Baltimore, was my grandfather."

8.

We chatted a little longer and then parted, amicably enough. I decided not to take the roundabout route, and retraced my steps back up the glen.

As I passed the lake, I glanced over again at the tiny island. For some reason it had become embedded in my mind that this was where they had found Matty Coyle. But my mind was now full of new thoughts and questions. Ray Conlon had mentioned that the trouble over Brannigan's mill had happened in the mid-thirties, around the time that Matty had drowned in the lake. What had Michael said? That when Matty drowned the Catholics said the local Prods who had done it. And the Prods had laid the blame with the Catholics. So was Matty's death connected in some way with the sectarian rivalries that erupted at that time? It would certainly have happened at roughly the same period. I would need to check further.

When I reached the farm the family had returned. As I entered the yard a gaunt figure, dark and awkward in an ill-fitting Sunday suit, was just emerging from the house. I recognised him by his slow, lolloping gait even from a distance. In spite of his name, Young Bob was now well into his sixties. He was my father's cousin and the present owner of Dernafleck Farm. He walked with a permanent stoop and always had to lift his head a little in order to look at you. He had a wizened face burnt dark from decades of work in the fields. But his eyes were bright and agile, and suggested a mind quick on the uptake. I had always thought that if Young Bob had been given the opportunity of education he would never have stayed on the land. He scrutinised me closely when he took my hand in his rough palm, as if trying to judge from my looks why I had come. For Young Bob, as for most country men, motives were important.

"Pity you weren't here earlier, Adrian. You could have come with us to the church. The Reverend Masterson just said a wee service, we laid a wreath on Old Bob's grave and then we had tea and cakes in the hall. It would have been good to have you there…"

"Thanks anyway, Bob," I said, "but I was taking the opportunity to revisit old haunts…"

A shadow crossed his wrinkled brown face. "You mean the glen? I never did know why you lads were so taken by that place. To us on the farm it was always a gloomy sink, full of bad odours and spirits. Never went down there myself, unless one of the heifers strayed into the trees. Never could stand the place…"

"Yes, I wanted to ask you about that, Bob," I said, falling step with him as we went back towards the house. "About the bad 'spirits' of the glen as you call them. Maybe you have some idea why it has such an evil reputation?"

He looked past me, towards the distant mountains, now bathed in a delicate pink glow from the sinking sun.

"Aye, it's got a bit to do with a character called Matty Coyle…but sure you know that already."

"You've been talking to Michael," I said.

"I have…Come in and sit down. We've eaten our fill today already. But Milly will make you some tea…and you'll take a bite to eat as well, no doubt."

I had only recently finished my tea and scones, but Milly emerged at that moment and repeated the invitation. I knew it was one I could not refuse, and was in any case glad to go in and take the weight off my feet. And ask more questions.

"So you remember Matty Coyle?" I asked Bob when we were settled by the kitchen range, each with a mug of Milly's strong tea beside us. The dogs padded round my chair, sniffing at me suspiciously.

"Do I remember him? Yes. Did I know him? Can't say I did really. He used to come here to the farm quite a bit, when I was a wain. You see, he was related to us…"

"By marriage, you mean? Matty was a Catholic surely…"

"No, not just by marriage. My father, old Bob, had a cousin, a girl who lived up near Feeny. And she married a Catholic from thereabouts, a very solid and respectable man, I believe, called Francis Coyle. And the wains, as always happens in these cases, were brought up Catholic…"

Bob paused while he took out his pipe and started searching in his pockets for a tin of tobacco.

"And Matty was one of those wains?" I asked.

He nodded as he lit the pipe and took his first puffs. "There were only two, Matty and his sister…"

"Yes, Michael mentioned there was a sister."

"Lottie, her name was…" Bob had suddenly become very pensive.

"And what became of her?" I asked, suddenly hopeful of a possible new avenue for investigation.

"Dunno," said Bob dismissively. "Probably dead this long time. In any case from what I've heard she was bats, went funny in the head when she was still a young thing and had to be sent away somewhere in the South…"

"In the South? Why the South?"

"They were Catholics, weren't they? She was sent to some home run by nuns, I think. No idea where it was…

He took the pipe out of his mouth and looked at me curiously. "Why does all this matter to you, anyway, young Adrian? Why all this sudden interest in Matty and his family?"

I hesitated a moment, wondering how much to let him know. "I found some things in my father's papers suggesting that...that he and Matty were friends at one stage."

Bob's whole attitude now seemed stiffer, less relaxed.

"Aye," he said slowly, "that they were. Or so ould Bob used to say. And it vexed him something terrible to speak of it..."

He went on chewing at the mouthpiece of his pipe, apparently not noticing that it had gone out.

"Why do you think that was, Bob? Why was old Bob vexed that Matty and my father were friends?"

Bob began the labour of refilling his pipe. "Don't get me wrong, Adrian," he said. "It wasn't just because Matty was Catholic...It was because he was...the ringleader of the trouble-makers."

"Trouble-makers?"

"The ones who made all the ballyhoo about the Upperfields shirt mill..."

So my suspicions had been right.

"Was that Brannigan's mill?" I asked quietly.

Young Bob was now becoming quite agitated himself.

"Aye, that's the one...Did you know they once planned to build a whole factory there, and bring in Catholics from Donegal?"

"You say Matty Coyle was some sort of ringleader?" I asked, ignoring his question.

"Aye, the organiser of it, the spokesman, the man who was at the head of it all...Had his picture in all the papers. Always making speeches and declarations, denouncing Beamish..."

"Beamish? Who was Beamish?"

"He was the local Unionist MP. This all happened before the elections, you know...There was an election campaign going on, and Beamish was the local MP for the Stormont parliament. But he was having a hard time from the zealous camp, particular from a character called Rev. Zechariah McIlroy..."

"A great name, but who was he?"

"He was a preacher, called himself a minister, from somewhere down around County Armagh, I believe...Anyway, McIlroy had started going round saying Beamish had gone soft on the Free Staters, because he'd taken part in a meeting in Dublin. McIlroy and his people made quite a stir about it...So Beamish knew he had to take a tough line, and the Brannigan affair gave him the opportunity."

This all seemed to fit in with what Ray Conlon had told me. With a very different gloss, of course.

"I see, and what did Beamish's tough line consist of?"

"Oh, he organised meetings and demonstrations calling for the Brannigan project to be cancelled."

"Only meetings and demonstrations?"

"Now there were indeed some shenanigans that went on…burning down of sheds and haystacks and that sort of thing. But it was done by both sides, and there was nothing to connect Beamish with that sort of stuff…"

I knew I had to tread carefully from now on, and tried to choose my words with caution.

"What were the Unionists so scared of? The factory would probably have employed some Protestants as well, wouldn't it? And even if most of the employees turned out to be Catholics, at least it would have kept them out of mischief, if you see what I mean. An employed man is less likely to go out and pick a fight with his Protestant neighbour…"

Bob took the pipe out of his mouth and snorted angrily. "You think Brannigan wanted to employ Protestants! Come off it, Adrian! This was just a scheme to bring more Catholics into the Protestant areas! You should have heard ould Bob on this subject. No two ways about it. The factory, and the houses for the workers, were all going to be built on Protestant land…"

"But was Upperfields Protestant land, Bob? From what I heard it was mainly Catholic, even then…"

"Aye, there was a little patch of them down by the bridge over the river. But all the land on this side of the river, where the factory was to be built, belonged to the Wallaces and McBeths. And Brannigan would have built houses all round it, and as I say, would have brought in people from the Bogside or from Donegal to live in them."

Bob was becoming more agitated by the minute. Milly poked her head in from the next room to tell him to keep his voice down.

"Were there really plans to import people from other districts?" I asked. "Do you know that for sure, Bob?"

"Oh, Brannigan put out all these statements about his factory being for the WHOLE community, and for EVERYONE's benefit. But you know what that lot mean when they say things like that! They mean: this is for us!"

Young Bob got up from his seat and shuffled to the window looking out on the yard. He stood there for several moments, sucking noisily on his pipe.

"No doubt they would have given a few of the houses to Protestants," he said finally, "just to say they weren't discriminating. Maybe five out of a hundred. If we were lucky!"

He went to the door and shouted to Michael across the yard, asking impatiently if anyone had seen to the new calf yet. Then the hunched frame disappeared somewhere, leaving me with my undrunk mug of tea and more questions than when I had started.

Young Bob's son, known as Young Robert, came into the kitchen a few minutes later carrying a pair of wellington boots. He greeted me warmly and sat down by the fire.

"Gone off and left you, has he?" he said cheerily, nodding towards the yard. "You must have been talking politics. It always puts him in a bad mood. But it won't last. He'll be friendly as they come by tomorrow...Talking of which, Adrian, there's a hooley tomorrow night, in the cricket club? Do you want to come?"

"What sort of a hooley?" I asked, without enthusiasm.

"Oh a disco, you know, for the young things. But it's a good chance for the rest of us to have a few pints...Come on, you'll enjoy it."

"I might pop in for an hour or so," I said reluctantly. "I have to go to Derry in the morning."

Discos were not really my scene. Nor, for that matter, were hooleys of any sort.

9.

In spite of what Ray Conlon had told me, I decided not to go back to the Coleraine Constitution, at least for the moment. Instead I headed in the other direction, to Derry, to see if the papers there were more obliging.

On the phone the deputy editor of the Foyle Herald had been suspicious at first when I explained my request. But he had no objection, he said, to my coming to search in the archives.

"As long as you come early in the day," he said, "and don't get in the way of deadlines. It's Tuesday tomorrow and we go to print the next day."

I arrived so early at the offices just off Shipquay Street that there was no one there but a secretary. Desy Quinn, the man to whom I'd spoken, arrived fifteen minutes later. He was as he had sounded, a pale-faced, suspicious man with straight dark hair and glasses.

"1935, you say? Yeah, it should be on fiche. They did them all a few years back. It's ages since I had reason to look back as far as that, though. Most enquiries are about the last ten years only...Sinead, take Mr...er...McCausland up to one of the fiche readers...you know, in the archives room on the third floor...and show him where the packet for 1935 is."

The room on the third floor had a view out over the roofs, across the walls and on to the tightly packed dwellings of the Bogside. The Catholic cathedral's smart neo-gothic rose high above them, looking back across the valley at the historic grey walls and the smaller, darker Protestant cathedral that sheltered behind them.

Sinead soon found the small packet of fiches for 1935 and left me to it.

At first I thought it was all a huge waste of time. The Herald at that time did not seem to do much coverage outside Derry city itself, or its hinterland in East Donegal. I had gathered from Ray Conlon that the events at Brannigan's mill had taken place in the summer and autumn, so I began searching in May. For the whole of that month, however, and much of June I found nothing but reports on cattle prices, young priests departing for the African mission field, and indignant statements by Nationalist politicians. No real sectarian confrontations, no fighting or shooting, certainly nothing in the way of suspicious deaths. Nor could I find any reference to Brannigan's shirt factory.

Then, in the edition dated 1st July, on the fifth page, bottom right corner, I finally found what I wanted.

U.S. ENTREPRENEUR VISITS COUNTY DERRY

'*Tuesday, 29th June—American businessman Al Brannigan today visited the planned site of an enterprise which he said would "bring hope to those who have no hope." Speaking after a morning spent walking around the muddy site in wellington boots, the Baltimore entrepreneur told your correspondent that he had left the district of Upperfields when he was six years old. "But it won't be so long before you see me again," he joked. The site overlooking the Banagher Burn five miles from Ballymully is being developed to house a textile factory which it is hoped will provide jobs for over 200 people. "These will be people from the district," said Mr Brannigan. "And though I believe there has been speculation about who they will be, I hereby give solemn assurances that they will represent a cross-section of the community at large"...*'

My reading was interrupted by the sound of footsteps on the bare wooden stairs outside and a knock on the door. I turned to see Sinead walking in and holding back the door for someone else. As the newcomer stepped into the room I recognised him at once. It was my acquaintance from the watermill teashop, Ray Conlon.

"Well, I didn't think you'd take up my suggestion so quickly," he said, offering a handshake.

"You forget! I already tried the Coleraine paper, and wasn't as lucky as you. So I thought if I got here ahead of you, you could intercede if I met the same response!"

He laughed. "Well, we're lucky they have two fiche machines, aren't we?"

"But only one set of fiches for 1935," Sinead pointed out. "Are you two guys looking for the same thing? It's funny, no one has asked for these fiches for years. Yet now two people come on the same day and ask for the same year!"

"Remarkable as it may seem," said Ray, "it is a total coincidence! And we're not even looking for the same thing...Or is that wrong?" He had noticed the look on my face.

"I don't know," I said. I hesitated about telling him what I had heard from Young Bob, and the possible connection between Matty Coyle and the Brannigan's mill dispute. I wanted to be sure I wasn't on the verge of discovering something sinister or embarrassing. "But I'm well into 1935, so if you start looking through the following year we can compare notes when we've finished. Might save a bit of time for both of us..."

He in his turn hesitated for a moment, frowning just a little. But then he shrugged.

"Why not? As you say, it may save time..."

Soon we were both settled by our fiche machines, scrutinising the endless column inches of newstype. We worked in silence, though every so often there was a faint grunt or whispered exclamation from my right as my companion made a note in the large jotting pad he had brought with him.

Finally, however, he pushed his chair back and said:

"I'm sorry, this isn't working. I need to see the material you're working on for any of this to make sense."

I could see what he meant. If he was researching the affair of Brannigan's Mill, he would need to go through the issues I was looking at. I decided it would be easier if I were frank with him.

"I think you're right," I said. "The whole thing did blow up in 1935. I've got it all here."

And then I told him who the "relative" was whose story concerned me, and what I had found out about him.

"Aha!" he said. "So we may be looking for the same thing after all..."

I showed him the report of Al Brannigan's initial visit to Upperfields, and then three more articles I had found focussing on the proposed mill at Upperfields. He peered over my shoulder, perusing the lengthy article I had up on the screen. It was dated 5th August and bore the title:

"Work starts on Upperfields mill."

"Hey presto!" he said, pointing. "There's your Matty Coyle!"

"Where?" I demanded, astonished.

He pointed to a faded photograph near the bottom of the page, and the passage directly beneath it.

'Mr Brannigan was welcomed at the Three Corners Inn at Upperfields by Father Frank Delaney and members of the Upperfields Development Association. The party is seen in the above photograph outside the Hotel after what Mr Brannigan described as a "truly memorable repast." Seen with Mr Brannigan (in the bowler hat, centre) and Father Delaney (to his right) are (from left to right) Messrs R. Maloney, D. McIlhanna, F. Donnelly, M. Coyle, C. Townsend and B. Mulligan, all members of the Development Association. Mr Brannigan returned to Derry City the same afternoon intending to travel on to Dublin, before spending some time with his family on the continent of Europe.'

"M. Coyle is the one three from the right," said Ray Conlon, still breathing down my neck.

I looked closely at the photograph. But the face of the man was, like the whole picture, very blurred. The only thing you could tell about him was that he was clean-shaven, unlike most of the other men in the photograph, and that he looked comparatively young, maybe in his late twenties or early thirties.

"Hm," I mused, staring in fascination at the hazy outline of the face. "M. Coyle...Yes, I suppose it could be him. But Coyle is a common name in County Derry and there must be dozens, if not hundreds of M. Coyles."

"In Upperfields? In 1935? Maybe, but let's look further..."

We split the 1935 wad of fiches in two and began looking for more clues. We had only been looking for another ten minutes or so, and had uncovered little more of significance, when Sinead arrived again from downstairs.

"Mr Conlon, there's a Mr Dougherty downstairs who's come to get you. And a few other people too."

Ray Conlon grunted something inaudible. Clearly he didn't want to give up the search. But with a sigh he handed his pile of fiches back to me. "Sorry, have to go and do the political rounds now," he said, and left the room.

I heard hearty voices and then laughter downstairs. Mr Dougherty had clearly not come alone. It sounded as if there was a whole welcoming party come to see the American visitor.

Intrigued, I ventured over to the door and listened. One voice stood out above the others, a deep, mellow voice which appeared to be trying to reassure Ray Conlon.

"Mr Conlon," the voice was saying, "you can have all the time in the world to study the Foyle Herald tomorrow or the next day. But we've laid on a few visits which I'm sure you wouldn't want to miss..."

If they were going to whisk my new acquaintance away so quickly I wanted to have another word with him. I wanted a contact address or number. I began to descend the stairs.

As I turned the corner and looked down at the dozen or so people now crowding into the newsroom, the first person to catch sight of me was Ray.

"Hey, Adrian! Come and meet Mr Dougherty! That's Councillor Dougherty, from your city council here..."

I smiled. "Well, not quite my council, since I've never lived in Derry..."

The man Ray indicated stood out from the others as physically as he had vocally. He was tall, well over six foot, and would have looked quite athletic had it not been for a slight stoop. And though he had a tanned, boyish face, I noticed he was going grey at the temples. He turned to me rather sharply, as if irritated by my unexpected arrival. But he recovered quickly and held out his hand.

"Joe Dougherty!" he said affably enough. "Known to my friends simply as Joe...and to my enemies as RRR, all the 'R's." He pronounced the last letter as an S, not a Z.

I must have looked totally bemused. There were several titters from around the room.

"RRR? That means Republican Rabble-Rouser," he explained, raising his eyebrows.

I didn't laugh because I didn't think it was funny. But I held out my hand, and after a moment he took it. His grip was firm. A bit too firm, I thought.

"And am I allowed to know your name?" he asked.

38

I noticed he had a very pronounced southern accent. And not from just from over the border, either. It was from much further south, I was sure.

"McCausland," I said, "Adrian McCausland."

He looked me over keenly, as if trying to guess what I was doing there.

"Adrian's also doing a bit of private research," Ray Conlon intervened. "Into a family related matter, not totally unconnected..."

"I'm sure," I interjected, "that Mr Dougherty has no interest in my family affairs. I'm sorry to have interrupted your meeting, Ray. I just wanted a contact address, or number. Then I'll go back up and continue..."

"Hey, no! Mr Dougherty and the...other members of the delegation were about to take me out to an Italian restaurant, to discuss my book and its...er... significance for the city. Why don't you come with us?"

There was an awkward silence. Then Joe Dougherty cleared his throat and said: "Well, er, I would have no objection myself, but seeing as it's a...well, a sort of official invitation, from the council as a whole, I'm afraid I'm not at liberty to invite Mr McCausland along." He looked at me pointedly, almost challenging me to protest. But I didn't. I had no real desire to join this particular dinner party.

"That all right, Ray. I'll go on looking through the fiches. We can have lunch or dinner some other time..."

"Well, that's fine then," said Joe Dougherty cheerily. "Shall we be on our way? By the way, Mr McCausland...is that a Derry name?"

"Well, there certainly are McCauslands round here," I answered. "My grandfather ran a business in the city until the fifties, but my cousin then sold it off, oh, some twenty-five years ago..."

"I've got it!" he said. "A stoneworks in the Abercorn Road!"

"That's it," I agreed.

"Aha," said Joe Dougherty knowingly. "So that's sorted that one out..."

"Yes," I replied pointedly. "We now know exactly where we stand."

Ray Conlon was looking on perplexed. He seemed annoyed at this meaningless exchange, but I patted him on the arm and said: "Don't worry, Ray. Local politics. You'd better go to your official function. No doubt we'll meet again some time..."

Ray gave me a telephone number, and the address of the house he had rented, not far from Dungiven.

"Why don't you call some time? We could compare notes again..."

Joe Dougherty ushered him out the door, and the other councillors, if that is what they were, filed out in their wake. They seemed an undistinguished lot, mostly schoolteachers or retired publicans, I guessed. Only one of them, a smallish, portly man with glasses and a shining bald head, honoured me with a nod of farewell. I smiled back at him.

The last to leave was a man who had been leaning casually against the side of the door, hands in his pockets. He gave a very different impression from the others. While nowhere near as tall as Joe Dougherty, this man also had an athletic build, though he was rather on the burly side, as if he had once been a boxer. His face was striking too. The colour of his skin was unusually dark, as if the man had Mediterranean ancestry or had spent a lot of time out of doors, maybe in the tropics. And he had hooded and, I thought, rather predatory eyes. His loose-fitting suit and yellow open-necked shirt were smart but casual, and he wore his greying hair long, hanging down over his collar. When the last of the council members had left the room he pushed himself off the doorpost and looked nonchalantly round the office, as if checking that no one was left behind.

Some sort of security man, I wondered, detailed to guard the city's elders? He certainly didn't look like a councillor, I thought. There was something altogether too sinister about him.

His watchful eyes crossed mine, and for a moment he fixed me with a look somewhere between amusement and contempt.

"Sorry you didn't get your nice meal," he said, and walked out after the others.

The accent, to my surprise, had been English. Somewhere from the south of England.

I began to climb back up to the fiche room, but as I came to the top of the stairs I heard footsteps behind me. Looking back, I saw the small man with glasses who had nodded a farewell. He glanced a little nervously over his shoulder, then continued up towards me, smiling.

"Hello, Mr McCausland. My name's Tim McCloskey. I hear that your personal research...may involve a man called Matty Coyle. Is that right?"

"Who told you that?" I asked in astonishment.

"Desy Quinn, the deputy editor...But am I right? Is that what you're looking for?"

I nodded, a bit coolly, annoyed that Quinn had been spreading it about.

"I might have something interesting to tell you," McCloskey continued. "I have to rush now, but perhaps we could meet and discuss it more fully on another occasion. Just give me a ring." He gave me a business card. "Or better still, give me your mobile number."

"Won't Mr Dougherty be annoyed if you don't consult him?" I said ironically, as I scribbled the number on one of his cards. Joe Dougherty had given the impression of someone who didn't like opposition.

"Oh don't worry about him," said Tim McCloskey, with a conspiratorial wink. "We have different interests. Different political parties, you see!"

And before I could say anything more, he disappeared back down the stairs.

10.

I decided to make the Banagher farm my base, for all the discomfort of Young Bob's hostility. It was, after all, very close to the scene of the original 'crime'. And Limavady, the closest town, might also throw up a few missing pieces of the jigsaw.

I woke early the next morning. The farm folk, of course, had been up and about their business for hours. I was relieved I didn't have to talk to Bob. Milly was the only one in the house, and she gave me breakfast alone in the kitchen, chattering merrily about the weather and the price of eggs. And then I was off.

It was only six miles to Limavady. I parked the car in a peaceful, tree-lined square in the centre of the town and walked to the public library.

One of the librarians, a helpful lady in glasses, showed me where I was most likely to find what I wanted.

I should have done this earlier, I thought, checked to see if anyone had recorded the story of Brannigan's mill in a magazine article or book. Perhaps I had assumed it was all too low key to merit academic research. And at first that assumption appeared only too well-founded. There was comparatively little local history in the library, except for scholarly works on Celtic tradition and a few rather tedious books on the Plantation. Certainly nothing on the period I was interested in.

But just as I was about to give up I found a slim volume put out by an institute for the study of conflict. Its title was: "Parades and Demonstrations: industrial and sectarian strife in Inter-war Ulster". I opened it and began flicking through the pages. I stopped at random half way through.

"1935," I read at the top of the page, "saw some of the worst sectarian rioting Belfast has ever seen..."

I found a desk and sat down, then started to read at the beginning of the chapter in question.

"Tensions increased across the province in 1931. A hall in Lurgan used by the Ancient Order of Hibernians (AOH) was daubed with provocative slogans, and on 12th July several fiery speeches were made at Orange parades...On the southern side of the border, where Orange parades had taken place since partition in counties Cavan, Monaghan and Leitrim, the IRA issued threats towards further parades of the Orange and Black orders...A Black Perceptory parade in Cootehill, Co. Cavan, *was stopped by a crowd after the IRA had declared it an 'imperialist-led Orange demonstration'. Speakers at a Black parade on the northern side of the border, at Aughnacloy, suggested this might justify reprisals. . ."*

Further down the same page there was more of the same.

"In Armagh a crowd attempted to stop the AOH parade reaching the town, and in Portadown two bus loads of Hibernians were chased by loyalists after they waved a green and white flag. . .The following day the B specials were mobilised to deal with continued disturbances in Portadown, and the Unionist 'News Letter' blamed 'Free State republicans' for parading through loyalist areas. . .In 1932. . .protesters tried to stop an AOH band from parading in Caledon on its way to a church service, and in retaliation a loyalist band was attack on the Crumlin Road in Belfast while returning from a commemoration of the Battle of the Somme. . ."

I flicked over to the next page and found the passage I had originally come upon.

". . .1935 saw some of the worst sectarian rioting Belfast has ever seen. Trouble began on St Patrick's Day when a nationalist band was attacked near High Street, apparently by a group who had been listening to speakers at the Custom's House. Later in the year the celebrations to mark the Jubilee of King George V increased tensions further, and from mid-June there were major disturbances. The Northern Ireland Home Secretary Dawson Bates took the drastic step of introducing a ban on all marches. However, this was rescinded four days later under pressure from the Orange Order. . .Parades on the Twelfth led to nine days of disturbances in the Docks area of the city. These resulted in the deaths of seven Protestants and three Catholics, while the occupants of four hundred and thirty Catholic and sixty-four Protestant houses were evicted. . ."

There was lots more like that. So much that I couldn't believe it. I had been brought up in happier times, and just hadn't realised there had been so much hatred in the past.

It was time to look more closely for information about the Brannigan case. I looked up the subject index at the rear of the volume. No, nothing for M. Coyle. But there were references to both Brannigan and Upperfields, on pages 76 and 78. Eagerly I turned the pages to see what the book said.

To my astonishment all the pages from 75 to 81 were missing. They had been neatly cut out, evidently with a pair of scissors.

I showed what I had found to the helpful librarian. She was clearly dismayed and called her superior. They tut-tutted over the damaged manuscript for some time, until I asked whether "Parades and Demonstrations" had been requested by anyone else in the recent past. That, I suggested, might tell us who was responsible.

Yes, the book had been borrowed only two weeks before. The head librarian remembered it well, because the gentleman had been an American. He had asked them to do some further research for him, and left his name.

Dr. R.S. Conlon. He was investigating his family history, he said.

"From a respectable East Coast university too!" she exclaimed indignantly. "And he was so polite!"

I smiled. "I wouldn't assume that Dr. Conlon is necessarily the guilty party. I know him a little, and...well, I don't think he's the sort of person who goes round snipping pages out of books. If he had wanted to keep a record of those pages, he could easily have asked you to photocopy them."

"But if it wasn't him, who else?" asked the chief librarian.

"That's a very good question," I said. "Dr. Conlon may have some idea. I hope to see him in the next few days...But I wonder, would it be infringing some rule on confidentiality, or would it be possible to look up what other materials Dr. Conlon had asked for when he was here?"

"In the circumstances," said the head librarian emphatically, "we'd be only too glad to break this gentleman's confidentiality..."

He had asked, as I suspected, for any material they could find on the Upperfields mill affair. The would-be owner, Al Brannigan, had been a relative of his, he had said. But they hadn't had time to start searching yet, said the Chief Librarian.

"We don't have that much time on our hands," she said rather huffily.

And the only other books Ray Conlon had consulted during his visit turned out to be two quite standard guidebooks on the North-West, so standard that he had not even borrowed them. I flicked through them, with the two ladies looking on. They both saw my disappointment.

"Nothing of interest, I take it," said the younger one.

"No, not much," I admitted.

But at that moment something fell out of the book I was holding and fell on the floor.

I picked it up. It was a faded cutting from a newspaper. It might have been used as a bookmark, I guessed, or simply have slipped between the pages as the previous reader thumbed backwards and forwards through the book.

"What is it?" they asked eagerly.

But it appeared to be nothing more than the obituary of a Catholic priest in the West of Ireland, taken from a Mayo newspaper called the *Western Argus*.

"Oh," said the assistant librarian, "so it's nothing to do with what you wanted."

Perhaps not, I thought. But as they went off to discuss what to do about the damaged book, I glanced at the clipping again. And something in the middle of the text caught my eye. Someone had faintly underlined a sentence with a pencil. And in the middle of that sentence were the words "Brannigan's mill".

I sat down again and began to read from the top. Underneath the photograph of an aged priest, smiling benignly at the camera, was the caption:

'FUNERAL OF REVERED AND GENTLE PRIEST'

'The funeral and interment took place this week of the late Father Teddy Delaney, who passed away on 15th March. Father Delaney was 88 years of age. He had spent his final years living at St Francis's College, Carrickdoo, after his retirement as a parish priest in 1972. A native of Co. Derry, Father Delaney had served parishes in Belfast, Co Sligo and here in Co Mayo, as well as in his native Derry. . .**Father Delaney was perhaps best known as the chronicler of the famous Brannigan's Mill affair, in which he was a direct participant.** As parish priest in the district of Upperfields, Co. Derry, he was a member of the Upperfields Development Association, formed in 1935, during the depression, to promote the interests of unemployed Catholics in the region. Part of his memoirs was published in the late sixties in this newspaper.

Requiem mass was said at St Brigid's, Carnloughey, by his friend and colleague for many years, Father Maurice O'Sullivan. In his address Fr O'Sullivan noted how unfortunate it was that Father Delaney had suffered from ill health in his later years, and was never able to complete his account of the stormy events he experienced at Upperfields. The funeral cortege. . .'

The rest was mostly details of the funeral. But I combed the obituary carefully, and right at the end I found something else.

'Father Delaney moved away from Upperfields parish soon after the Brannigan affair. Some said this was at the insistence of the RUC, because of the role he had played in the Development Association. The controversial and outspoken Unionist MP Cyril Beamish had accused Father Delaney of 'supporting violence', a charge which the gentle and much-loved priest always denied. According to his friend Father O'Sullivan, indeed, some Nationalists were also critical of Fr Delaney, even accusing him of collaborating with the RUC and the Six County authorities. His critics charged him specifically with seeking the disbandment and deportation of the team of Security Men brought over by Al Brannigan from America, to protect the site of the proposed shirt factory from attacks by loyalist gangs. It is tragic, Father O'Sullivan told us, that these false accusations from both sides should have tarnished the good name of such an honest and conscientious priest. . .'

I searched the text further, but there were no more references to Upperfields.

***

At that moment my mobile rang.

"Hello there, this is Tim McCloskey," said the voice. "You remember, we exchanged phone numbers, in the Foyle Herald offices. . ."

"Oh yes…"

"I thought I'd get on to you…You see, I've got information that might be very interesting for you…Did you know that Matty Coyle had a sister?"

"Yes, I did know that," I said a little impatiently.

"And did you know she was still alive?"

The news was meant to impress me. And it did. "Is that so now?" I gave a low whistle. "So where is she? Still in the Republic?"

"No, she's here. Here in Derry. Living in the Bogside."

I was astonished. "Is Ray Conlon aware of this?"

"No, not that I'm aware."

"Or Joe Dougherty?"

"I haven't asked him…But then I don't speak to him very often."

I was still mystified. "So why are you telling *me* all this, Mr McCloskey, rather than Ray Conlon? After all, he seems to be an honoured guest of the city."

"Mhm," he agreed. "Let's just say I trust you more than I trust him. He's altogether too much under the wing of Councillor Dougherty…"

I said I knew what he meant. "Do you have an address, though? A telephone number? Can I go and see her?"

"I'll take you there myself. Can you come into Derry this afternoon? Three o'clock say?"

II.

"You know she's loopy, don't you?" said Tim McCloskey as he drove me across the Foyle. We had met at a car park in the Waterside, east of the river, and were now heading for Lottie's home, which he told me was in the middle of the Bogside. "Locked away for years, she was."

I glanced out the window. We were over the two-layered metal bridge and had turned left to skirt the city centre. "Locked away where?" I asked.

"Oh, some religious institution in the south. Galway or Mayo, I think. She didn't get coming back to Derry until she was about forty. She's lived here in the Bogside ever since, in a cousin's house. They were the only people willing to take her in..."

We were now entering the area of narrow streets and cramped houses which had gained fame, or notoriety, over the years as the spiritual centre of Derry republicanism. I was nervous, very nervous. It wasn't so much that it was a republican area and everyone would be able to see I didn't belong. It was more that I was about to meet a person who might well know what had happened on the night sixty years ago when her brother died. Was I going to find out something it would probably have been better not to know?

We passed some modern flats and turned into a long road of identical, terraced houses, rising slowly towards St. Eugene's cathedral. There was a faint haze in the air and the pungent odour of smoke from domestic fires, a somehow nostalgic smell that reminded me of my youth. The house we were heading for was half way up the street.

A pale, mournful looking woman opened the door for us, and immediately melted back into the hallway.

"The cousin's daughter," McCloskey murmured to me as we followed. "Her name's Shenagh." I was beginning to warm to the little man with the balding head. He had a sense of humour, and was the most cheerful person I had met since I'd come over for my father's funeral. Shenagh was waiting by the door into the front room. She nodded towards it, her manner off-hand and indifferent, almost hostile.

When I entered the room, at first I thought there was no one there. I looked round the cramped but tidily furnished parlour, at the empty sofa and armchairs, the fading brown wallpaper and the standard pictures of mountains and white cottages. In one corner of the room, to my surprise, was a piano.

And then I saw her. She was over by the window, in an austere old armchair covered in faded flowers. The chair was placed at an angle, so that she could see up the street, and her gaunt silhouette stood out sharply against the light of the sun. The sight of her had a strange effect on me, as if the thin, motionless figure was not a real person. As I drew closer I saw that her head had something distinctly bird-like about it. It seemed to be cocked to one side, on the end of a delicate, thin neck, with the hair long and unkempt, tied loosely with a single green ribbon. Then, as I moved round to one side of her and my eyes grew accustomed to the light, I caught sight of her features.

It was perhaps not as old a face as I had imagined. But it did carry very visible signs of a difficult life, of cruelty and neglect, and of long remembered pain. Lottie was probably no more than seventy-five, but her eyes were sunk deep in dark hollows, and her mouth twitched constantly as if there were some hot coal inside it which she had to continuously keep moving so it would not burn her tongue.

The eyes were the most intriguing part of her face. They were of a milky blue and for much of the time wore a distant expression, like the windows of an absent soul whose mind had been worn out over the years and now resided in a far distant country. Only as she turned her head slightly toward me, and saw a new and unfamiliar face, did they suddenly brighten with a spark of curiosity. Then they settled on me, and narrowed, as if trying to burn a way into my thoughts. Slowly I gained the impression of a person who, whatever emotional or psychological damage she had suffered over the years, still possessed elements of a keen intelligence. It was a face which I would not have immediately associated with a simple farming girl—especially one who had been shut away for many years in an institution.

"Lottie," said Shenagh slowly and deliberately, "you have some visitors."

Lottie raised her eyes questioningly as Tim bent down over her. Taking her hand in his own he said, "Lottie, you remember me? I'm Councillor McCloskey, and I've been round before, if you may remember, because you and Shenagh had a problem with the drains."

Lottie immediately seemed to lose interest. Her head sank back to its previous, bowed position, and her eyes stared back out towards a group of children playing in the street. Her gaze was so fixed that I began to wonder if she had actually lost the power of sight.

"And I've brought with me someone you'll be interested to meet. This is Mr McCausland, Adrian McCausland, and he says he may be related to you."

The curious bird's head stirred. The eyes flickered, but even as I sat down in the chair opposite her, they continued to look past me towards the children playing outside.

For a moment I lost heart. Would this, after all, prove to be a wasted journey? It looked very much as if Lottie had very little left inside that woolly head

THE TRAGIC FATE OF MATTY COYLE

of hers, and I began to doubt if she could even understand what we were saying to her.

For at least a minute we just sat there, in silence. Then, quite unexpectedly, Lottie spoke.

"This the one says he knew Matty?" she asked. A frail voice, curiously high-pitched, floating on the air.

I was flabbergasted. No one had mentioned Matty.

"No," said Tim patiently, "he didn't know Matty. His father did."

The long neck moved back a little, almost like that of a turkey reacting to someone who has come too close.

"What was his father's name?"

"Lottie," I said gently, "my father's name was Lexie. Lexie McCausland. Did you ever, by any chance, meet him?"

She still wasn't looking at me, but I could swear the name meant something to her. Her soft blue eyes flickered again, then seemed to fix on a spot on the house opposite and stare at it unrelentingly. I now had absolutely no doubt that she was anything but blind. There was something in those eyes, a sparkle, a can-niness, which told me she saw things more clearly than most. And understood who I was only too well.

Yet when she finally spoke it was in a wooden voice. "No, didn't know him," she said, and turned away to gaze down the street at some children playing.

"But he was a friend of your brother Matty!" I exclaimed. "Several people have told me that..."

Shenagh had come back into the room and began signalling to me, with a disapproving look, to desist.

I felt helpless and frustrated. "Do you mean, Lottie, that you don't know who my father was," I asked, "or just that you never actually met him yourself?"

She turned back, and for the first time she looked straight at me. Something had hardened in her eyes, become more definite. Again I had the impression of a wily determination. Her lips formed into a tremulous smile.

"Likely he was one of those in the ructions at Upperfields," she said, her smile slowly spreading.

I leaned forward. "Yes, Lottie, I think he was. But what I'd like to know is: how was he involved in those ructions?"

The smile disappeared from her face. She made no answer. She just sat there now, once again looking straight past me at the houses opposite.

"Likely he was the one that was with Matty when he disappeared. Aye, he would have been that one..."

This shook me, I have to admit. I thought of what Young Bob and Michael had told me back at Banagher. "You think my father was with Matty on the night...that he died?"

49

"Aye, most likely," she said with a sort of disdainful sniff. "There was just the two of them, Matty and this other boy…What did you say your name was?"

"Adrian," I said, "Adrian McCausland…"

"No, it wasn't him. But he had a name like that…"

"That's my name, Lottie. My father's name was Alexander."

She looked puzzled.

"To his friends he was known as Lexie."

She fixed me with her eyes, and this time I was sure she was sending me a message. It was almost as if she wanted to say: 'You're close to the truth, but you'll have to work harder to get it out of me.' Yet all she actually said was:

"Aye, that's the one. That's the one that took Matty off into the night…"

When I heard it, that sentence sent a pain through my chest so sharp it was as if she had stabbed me. I don't know what I had expected from Lottie, but it certainly wasn't this. Basically she had confirmed my worst fears. My father had gone off somewhere with Matty on the night that he died, and they had been, it seems, alone.

"Matty trusted him, you know," she broke out, with more emotion now in her voice. "He was the only one of them Matty trusted. That's why he went with him…"

I was struggling to make sense of what she was saying. "He was the only one of whom, Lottie? Who were *they*?"

"The only one of them Prods…"

"And did my father…Lexie…invite Matty to go with him?"

She nodded, still keeping her eyes fixed on me.

"And where did they go?"

"I don't rightly know, but I think it was down to the glen…Aye, they were going to the glen. I heard Matty say something about the mill house. But I wasn't supposed to know. They didn't tell me anything. You see, I was only young, and such a bold girl…"

My heart had fallen to somewhere around my feet. There didn't seem much point in going on. It was lucky, I thought, that Lottie hadn't spoken to anyone else, because every word she said only strengthened the suspicions that my father's role in the affair had not been an innocent one. Indeed it seemed that he, as Matty's trusted friend, might well have been the one who had set Matty up for whatever happened to him down in the glen, near the mill…

"They killed him, you know," Lottie said suddenly. "Aye, they killed him…"

"But who were they, Lottie?" I asked again, a sudden faint ray of hope in my heart. She was talking in the plural now. So evidently my father had not been the only one involved.

But she looked away from me immediately, and would say no more. No more, in any case, that was coherent. Her head dropped, and she started mumbling to herself and letting out strange groaning noises. Then her voice began to change. It became a whimper, and then a long, thin wail. Her face began to convulse, and her head started bobbing strangely backwards and forwards. I realised she was crying.

"Now you've gone and upset her," said Shenagh, stepping forward and kneeling to put her arm round the old woman. "You've gone and upset her real bad, as I knew you would, with your questions...Why can't you all just leave her alone?"

"Why," I asked in surprise, "has someone else been asking her questions?"

"Too many of you, far too many," said Shenagh, pulling the blanket up round Lottie's shoulders and trying to comfort her.

"Who was it?" I persisted, suddenly feeling anger. "And when?"

Shenagh just shook her head. After a few minutes she got up from Lottie's side. The old woman continued to rock backwards and forwards in her chair. Shenagh leaned against the dresser and put one hand up beside her face. She looked harassed and unhappy.

"Was one of them an American, for instance?" I asked.

"I think you should go now," said Shenagh, biting her lip. "I only agreed to let you see her because of Mr McCloskey here..."

"Shenagh, let the man ask his questions," Tim put in. "His father just died there recently, and he just wants to know about the old man's past, what he got up to in the old days..."

To our surprise and consternation, Shenagh burst into tears. "I'm sorry, Mr McCloskey...You see, there's been others here, asking questions. And telling us not to..."

At that moment a car door slammed shut outside in the street, not far from the house, and a moment later a figure passed the window. Shenagh put her hand over her mouth.

"Oh God," she murmured, "it's him!"

12.

"Quick!" Shenagh urged us. "With any luck he didn't see you. Go into the back room, and don't say a word! Please, Mr McCloskey. For my sake, and Lottie's."

We did as we were asked without protest. As Shenagh closed the door after us the doorbell went, a long insistent ring. She went to answer it. I stood close to the door leading into the hall, listening intently.

"Oh, it's you, Mr. eh...I didn't rightly catch your name."

"My name's Hill, Mrs Kelly, my name's Hill. Now are you going to let me in?"

The voice had an ingratiating tone, but there was no mistaking the threat it carried. The accent struck me as odd. It was a curious mixture of local Ulster and English, as if the speaker were an Englishman who had spent a lot of time living in Ireland, or possibly a local who had gone to live in England when he was young. The intonation was almost pure cockney, but some of the words and phrases could only have been heard in County Derry.

I suddenly realised that I knew this voice. It was the man who had spoken to me in the Foyle Herald offices. The 'security man' with the athletic physique and the natty clothes.

"Lottie's in the front room, as usual," Shenagh was saying. She was no more than a few feet away from me now, in the narrow entrance hall.

"It wasn't actually dear Lottie I wanted to speak to," said the man's mockingly polite voice. "It was your good self. Now a little bird told me recently that you'd been talking to that Tim McCloskey again."

"Tim McCloskey's an old friend of my father's," she said defiantly. "I can't keep him from calling round."

"Ah, so he has been calling round, has he?"

There was a short pause.

"He came the other day..."

"Oh I think he's been here more recently, don't you? You see, I think that's his car out there in the street. The old shabby thing that I parked beside. He wouldn't still be round, would he?"

"Yes...I mean, he called here half an hour ago...Then he went off on his rounds, I think, to visit people in this area. After all, he is a city councillor..."

"Indeed he is, Mrs Kelly. Indeed he is. So what did he want with you today? Bring anyone else with him, did he?"

"There was a man with him…but I don't know who he was."

There was a tense silence, suggesting the newcomer, Hill, was not convinced.

"He went off with Mr McCloskey," Shenagh added.

"Mind if I wait here for them?"

There was another silence. "I don't know if they're going to call back. But you can stay if you like. I'll make you a pot of tea and you can sit in the kitchen…"

I heard Tim, beside me, draw a sharp intake of breath. But then Hill said:

"Well that's mighty kind of you, Mrs Kelly, but actually I've changed my mind. I won't stay today, thank you. Got a few things to do in the vicinity myself, I have…But I just want to make one thing very clear, Mrs Kelly. The next time jolly old Tim McCloskey comes calling, tell him to clear off quick, will you, and not come calling again…Because if it comes to my ears that he's been bothering poor old Lottie here, him and this other geezer that's with him, just let him know something very nasty might happen."

"Are you threatening me?" asked Shenagh sharply.

"I'm not threatening you, my dear," Hill replied, his voice rising and losing something of its suave tone, "and I'm not threatening dear Lottie neither, nor big fat Tim nor his friend…I ain't threatening no one. But tell him from me that if he comes again then something really nasty, and I mean that, will happen to one or other of you."

And almost at once we heard the front door slam.

We came out of the back room and found Shenagh leaning against the banisters, trembling and weeping silently into her apron.

"Who was he, Shenagh?" I asked. "Who was that bastard?"

She wiped her eyes.

"His name's Sean Hill," Tim answered from behind me. "And you're right, he's a complete bastard. I don't know exactly who he works for. One of the smaller republican factions, I suspect. But he's also been known to work for Dougherty. You may have seen him at the Foyle Herald…"

"Yes," I said grimly, "he told me before he went out how sorry he was I was missing the nice meal…"

"That sounds like him all right. Someone you want to avoid if at all possible."

We crept into the front room again and I went to the window to try and get a glimpse of Hill. His burly frame was fast receding down the street.

"He sounded like an Englishman," I said.

"Brought up in England," Tim replied. "His parents left Derry when he was a youngster. They were a mixed family, I believe, father a Protestant, mother a Catholic. They moved to England when the troubles began. But Sean came back, and was soon mixed up with republican paramilitaries. They say his English accent was very useful when it came to under-cover work...posing as a British squaddie, for instance. And then there are those that say..."

He paused.

"Who say what, Tim?"

"Who say that he's really working for the Brits. You know, trying to in-filtrate the republican movement...Certainly there are quite a few republicans who don't like or trust him. Partly because of his English accent...But whoever he's working for, when there's trouble brewing our Sean's always likely to be in it somewhere..."

"So what's his game? Why is he threatening Shenagh and Lottie? And us too, it seems..."

"Dunno. Your guess is as good as mine..."

We watched Hill until he reached a sporty but aging green car, glanced furtively round him in several directions, and got in. A moment later he pulled out and drove at speed up the hill past the house. We both shrank back from the window.

"Yes," said Tim again. "Definitely someone you need to avoid."

13.

The cricket clubhouse at Banagher was a low L-shaped building. I remembered going there once or twice in the old days, to watch one of the keenly contested matches which were a feature of North-West cricket. The pitch was situated on the edge of the glen a mile or so up from the farm. Quite a few balls had been lost, I had heard, when over-enthusiastic sloggers had launched them over the line of netting at the "glenside end" into the trees.

But it was winter now, and the clubhouse had taken up its out of season function as a social centre, at least for one half of the community. As I parked in the over-crowded gravel space outside I noticed that the car next to mine was a sleek, powerful sports model, not your normal family limousine. A dog had slunk out of the darkness and was sniffing at its paintwork suspiciously. Farmers! I said to myself. They complain all the time about being overtaxed, but some of them could still afford machines like this!

The longer leg of the L had been taken over for their disco by what Young Robert had called the "young things". This group seemed to include everyone from girls of thirteen to fairly rotund men well into their thirties. They were jumping, hopping and wiggling around to the relentless beat of some throbbing music, against the garish background of flashing, blinking disco lights.

Round the corner, sheltered from the direct blast of the music, was the bar. This is where I found Young Robert, installed with a boisterous group of under-forties. Among the loud voices and flushed faces, however, one figure stood out for its reserve and sobriety. This was a man of above average height who stood stiffly to one side, his right hand clutching a pint glass, his left stuffed deep in a trouser pocket. He was dressed in dark green blazer and striped tie. This, and the neatly groomed moustache, gave him a self-consciously military bearing.

"This is Mervyn Ritchie," Young Robert introduced him as I went round the group shaking hands. "Mervyn is our protection round here, in these difficult times." He leaned over to me and added, with a conspiratorial whisper: "He's the Detective Sergeant at Limavady, but he lives just up the road…so we can sleep peacefully at night."

DS Ritchie grunted. "I don't know if I give you protection, Robert, or whether it's the other way round." He had a surprisingly high-pitched voice, which somehow undermined the air of authority he affected.

"Glad to meet you," I said, holding out my hand.

He took it limply, but didn't reciprocate my greeting. "What brings you to these parts?" he asked.

"Oh Adrian's come to investigate the Brannigan mill affair," Young Robert announced. "You know, the ructions in the thirties. He thinks his father was involved in it somehow."

There was a momentary silence among the group, and the pounding beat of the music seemed suddenly much louder.

"And how was it that your father was involved?" asked Mervyn Ritchie, eyeing me keenly as he took a sip of his beer.

"I'm not sure. That's what I want to find out. But somehow he was involved with a fellow called Matty Coyle, who later was killed. Or at least died in mysterious circumstances."

The silence persisted. Everyone, for some reason, seemed to be looking at Ritchie, as if expecting him to take a lead.

"Matty Coyle," said the detective sergeant. "Wasn't he the leader of the Nationalist vigilantes?"

"He was chairman of what they called the 'Upperfields Development Association'," I answered.

There were a number of nervous laughs from the surrounding group. "The original UDA!" somebody quipped. Mervyn Ritchie, however, did not seem amused.

"They called it a Development Association at first," he said, barely trying to conceal his disdain, "but then later the Catholics started calling it a **Defence** Association. That's the way they saw it...But can I ask, Mr McCausland, what exactly was the relationship between your father and Coyle?"

He was beginning to irritate me with his questions. "What is this?" I said to him, trying to smile. "An interrogation?"

"No," he said, "it's a perfectly normal question. Why was your father 'involved', as you put it, with someone like Matty Coyle?"

"I don't know. That's what I'm hoping to find out. All I do know is that they were distantly related. And they were, in a sense, colleagues. Both were teachers."

"Colleagues?" Mervyn Ritchie raised his eyebrows. "What, at the same school?"

"No, obviously not. Matty Coyle was a Catholic..."

"Yet they were related?" He was relentless with his questions, his suspicions. Maybe it's because he's a detective, I thought. Or maybe it was just because he had a suspicious mind.

"A mixed marriage somewhere in the family," I said.

There were several moments of silence. Broken by Ritchie.

"There seems to be a great surge of interest recently in the Brannigan mill affair," he commented. "A couple of months ago some relative of Brannigan's over in America submitted a request for the police archives to be opened up..."

"Ah," I said with interest, "was that someone called Ray Conlon, by any chance, from a college in Baltimore?"

He looked annoyed for some reason. "Yes, I think it was. How did you know?"

"I met him yesterday. Down at the mill house in Banagher Glen. He seems to have gone some way in his researches..."

"Has he indeed?" said Ritchie, now clearly displeased.

"Did you allow him to see your archives?" Young Robert asked.

Ritchie shook head vehemently. "Of course not. Why should we give someone like that access to..."

"To what?" I asked pointedly.

"To things which are better left the way they are, dead and buried," he said emphatically.

"You mean...like Matty Coyle," I said, a little too quickly, and immediately regretted that I had. Suddenly there was real tension in the air. Mervyn Ritchie seemed to rise two or three inches in the soles of his shoes, and he appeared to look past me at some point high up in the corner of the room.

"I think, Mr McCausland," he said very deliberately, "that you'd be well advised not to dig too deeply in your researches. People round here don't like people raking up dirt about the past, you know. And I think you should be particularly careful, in your position..."

"I'm sorry, I'm not sure I understand what you mean by...'my position'?"

He leaned confidently against the bar, with a small and slightly twisted smile on his face. "When the request for access came from Conlon I was asked by my superiors to look back at the circumstances of the case, and I found a few very interesting things about it..."

He paused, evidently for dramatic effect.

"Go on," I said, "tell us."

"Your father was Lexie McCausland?"

I nodded.

"Well, perhaps you weren't aware of this, but your father was the last person to be seen with Matty Coyle before he was found dead."

There was a stir among the circle of people standing in our group. I don't know whose side they were on. Probably about evenly divided between Ritchie and myself. But everyone saw that Ritchie now had me in a corner.

And he clearly wanted to press his advantage home. "I'll tell you another thing," he said. "I don't think your friend Ray Conlon would have been too pleased with some of things I uncovered."

"Why's that?" I asked coolly.

"Well, you see there were a lot of things about this case that the Nationalists might not want revealed...Did you know, for example, that Brannigan brought over from America a whole gang of thugs. There were about a dozen of them. He didn't call them thugs, of course. I think he used the term 'Security Men'. But the police in America were able to inform the RUC that they were hoodlums, very much part of the criminal underworld..."

"You mean the mafia!" said one of the onlookers.

"Mafia, gangsters, crooks, whatever," said Ritchie.

"Yeah, I heard they all had Italian names," volunteered someone from along the bar. "Wasn't their leader called something like...Peckinpaw?"

"Peccatini," Ritchie corrected him. The name stirred something in my mind, but I couldn't for the moment think why.

"And were they active?" I asked. "I mean, were they actively involved in any of the violence?"

Ritchie gave me a slightly condescending look, as if secretly pleased I had at least shown some interest in his version of events. "There's no doubt they were. Beamish, the Unionist MP, finally managed to have them sent home. He persuaded the Home Secretary to threaten them with deportation."

"So they just went?" asked Robert.

"It seems so. And soon afterwards the whole thing blew over."

Ritchie's version seemed all too simple. I stared gloomily for some moments at a brightly lit advertisement for Danish beer. "Did they leave before Matty Coyle's death?" I asked. "Or afterwards?"

Mervyn Ritchie set his empty glass down, very deliberately, on the counter. "I don't know," he said. "Perhaps you'll be able to find that out for yourself."

And with a few crisp waves of his hand he took his leave, pushing his way through the heaving bodies and flashing lights of the disco.

"You don't seem to have made a friend there, Adrian," Young Robert commented.

I tried to laugh it off. "Certainly your DS Ritchie doesn't take kindly to having his word questioned," I said.

"No," Young Robert agreed, "he likes to think he's an authority on just about everything."

14.

"They call this Saltimbocca!" exclaimed Ray Conlon. "It's more like Irish stew!"

Tim Devlin laughed. "Sure what do you expect? The restaurant's called Francorelli's, but that's only because the owner's name is Frank O'Reilly!"

"What are you complaining about?" I asked. "It's very good Irish stew!"

My companions laughed. But then I saw the smile freeze on Tim's face. I was vaguely aware that at the other side of the restaurant the glass doors had opened and someone had entered. I turned in that direction, to see who it was had caught Tim's attention, but whoever it was had moved behind a column and was being seated by one of the waiters near the window.

"Who is it?" I asked him.

"Oh, nobody," he replied vaguely. "Somebody I thought I recognised. But maybe I was mistaken..."

The waiter brought the desert course, and Tim and Ray set about their tiramisu with obvious relish. But for me the pleasure and good humour of the evening had somehow lost their sparkle. My thoughts kept returning to the un-identified person sitting behind the pillar on the far side of the room.

Tim and Ray had ordered coffee and were now discussing the latest politi-cal row in the city council. If Gaelic street names were to be allowed in the Bog-side and Creggan, should the loyalist areas on the Waterside be allowed to have them in Lollands Scots? Ray Conlon found the whole thing highly amusing.

"Surely it's just English with half the words spelled wrong?" he said, chuck-ling.

Tim was inclined to agree with him. "But if they want it that way, why not allow it? It's not harming anyone..."

I got up and left them to it, on the pretext of searching for the gents. I knew perfectly well it was in the corner near our table, but deliberately went to ask the barman near the door. I wanted to get a glimpse of the man behind the column.

The table was empty. I could have sworn that nobody had emerged from behind the pillar since the man had come in. But now there was nothing there but an empty whisky glass, a crumpled napkin and a rolled up newspaper with a partly finished crossword.

"I'm sorry," I asked the man behind the bar, "but did you see where the man went who was sitting here?"

"Oh he just came in for a quick whisky, sir," answered the barman. "Then he paid up and went."

I glanced through the window out on to the street. It was virtually empty. There was a line of cars parked on the far side, but apart from that very little of any note. I scanned one car after the other, watching for some telltale movement, or perhaps the glow of a cigarette in the darkness. But there was nothing.

"Did you have some business with him?" asked the barman, clearly intrigued by my interest in the departed man.

"Er, no, no," I said hurriedly. "Just thought I might have known him…Was he someone you know yourself?"

The man behind the bar shook his head. "No, complete stranger to me." But he was smiling to himself, as if his answer wasn't as honest as it might have been.

I returned to the table. Ray Conlon had ordered a cognac for each of us, and in spite of my protestations insisted that we stay for a while and enjoy a couple of the small cigars he had laid on the table.

"I have to drive back home," I protested helplessly.

But the two of them sat there, grinning up at me. What could I do? I shrugged and sat down.

By the time we finally paid and walked out into the cool of the evening, the street was totally deserted. Tim had his car parked only a few yards from the entrance. He was giving Ray a lift back to his hotel on the Waterside. I clasped both of them warmly by the hand, and Ray gave me a rather drunken bear hug.

"Not a bad guy, is he, Tim? For a Prod, that is…"

We all laughed, and I waved goodbye and turned to walk away.

I had parked just round the corner from the restaurant. The glow of the floodlit Guildhall rose over the nearby roofs, but here in the quiet side street there was only a single stark lamp, further down near the quays. Its feeble light merely accentuated the darkness of the shadow-filled recesses along the winding street. It was difficult to make out the colour or make of the cars parked along the pavement, and I peered at several before I located the right one.

I had just taken out the keys from my pocket and was searching for the lock when I became aware of a presence just behind me.

I turned sharply and found myself facing a tall figure in a dark jacket and woolly hat.

"How was the macaroni then?" the figure said in a whimsical, faintly mocking voice.

I straightened up and peered at the newcomer. His face was in shadow, but I knew the voice.

"Oh, did I startle you? Coming out of the dark like that? Do forgive me." It was the same ironic, mocking tone I had heard in the offices of the Foyle Herald. And in Shenagh Kelly's front hall.

"If you have a moment?" the voice went on. "I won't keep you for more than a minute or two…"

Did I have a choice?

"What is it you want?" I asked. I glanced nervously back towards the brightness of the Strand. But the man had in the meantime moved round to that side of me, and leaned nonchalantly against the side wall of the restaurant. For the first time I noticed he had a cigarette in his hand. He lifted it slowly and took a long pull. For an instant I caught a glimpse of his heavy jowled face and thick, dark eyebrows.

"Have we met before?" I asked him.

He blew out the smoke and cocked his head in a strange, questioning way. "Why yes, don't you remember? At the newspaper office the other day. I think you were doing some…research, was it?"

I nodded. "Ah yes," I said. "But I didn't catch your name on that occasion."

"Sean Hill, Mr. McCausland. My name's Sean Hill. I'm surprised you haven't heard of me…in the course of your researches."

I shrugged. "Should I have? Are you an expert on civil strife in the 1930s?"

He affected a laugh. "No, no. Oh dear me no. No, it's just that I'm quite a well known figure…in local circles."

I was growing impatient. "Look, could we come to the point? It's getting a bit late for casual conversations on the street."

"Indeed it is, Mr. McCausland. Indeed it is…As you say, let's get to the point. The point is that I've been given a message for you."

He waited for me to react. I said nothing, so he went on.

"A friend of mine wishes it to be known that he's willing to help you in your researches. Though there would be certain conditions attached."

Again I said nothing.

"Aren't you interested in knowing more?"

"Who is this friend of yours?"

"Oh that I'm not at liberty to divulge. But he's somebody who could give you valuable information about…what was it called? The Brannigan Mill affair?"

I thought for a moment. "Why can't he come and see me himself?"

"He prefers not to," was the reply, delivered with finality.

"So how is he going to give me this…'valuable information'?"

"I would be the intermediary."

Of course. Why had I bothered to ask?

The tone of his last two replies gave me to understand that Hill was beginning to lose patience. He took another, long pull on his cigarette.

"Can you give me any idea of the nature of the information on offer?" I asked.

He pushed himself off the wall and threw his cigarette on the pavement, where he stamped on it with studied thoroughness.

"Oh, it would be in the nature of general indications, shall we say…as to where to look and not to look."

I looked at him questioningly. "For example?"

"For example, that you needn't go bothering poor Lottie Coyle. She's an innocent party in all this. She definitely knows nothing that would be of use to you…At least, that's what my friend says."

I raised my eyebrows. "Really?" I said. "Well, that's interesting…I'll bear that in mind."

I wanted to say something stronger, but I held back.

"So if I wanted to take up your offer, how would we do it? Would we have to meet again, somewhere else?"

He didn't answer. He seemed to be looking blankly into the dark, his hands stuffed deep into his coat pockets.

"How would I get in touch with you?" I pressed him.

He stirred, as if he had momentarily forgotten my presence.

"You wouldn't," he said. "I'd get in touch with you."

And without further ado, Hill turned and made off in the direction of the quayside.

"Don't you have a telephone number at least?" I called after him.

There was no reply, and a moment or two later he was gone.

15.

"Mr. Beckton is in Belfast all today," the secretary, Miss McFarlane, came back to me on the phone. "And he's going to Dublin and then London for the rest of the week."

I knew it wasn't true. I had been in Coleraine since early that morning, and had stationed myself near his office, on one of the wooden benches that lined the embankment, looking out over the river. The editor of the 'Constitution' had duly arrived fifteen minutes later, parked his car on the reserved space further along the embankment, and gone into the building.

"So he doesn't want to see me," I said drily.

At the other end of the line she hesitated. "Well...it's not that he doesn't want to see you, sir. It's just that he's busy...away on business, for the rest of this week."

"And next week?"

Again she hesitated. "Er...well, if you liked, we could arrange an interview for next week."

"That won't be necessary," I said, and put the phone down.

I exited the phone booth and strode rapidly back along the embankment. A lone sculler appeared from under the bridge, battling against the current. It was so strong that he was well behind me by the time I reached the newspaper offices.

I walked through the main door and up the stairs.

"Excuse me!" called a voice from the reception desk near the entrance. But by then I was at the top of the stairs and turned right towards the editor's bureau.

Miss McFarlane rose from her seat when I entered. "Good morning," I said, pulling her a smile as I walked past into Beckton's sanctum.

He was at his desk, poring over some documents spread across his desk. Miss McFarlane rushed in after me.

"Mr. McCausland, you can't just go barging..." She seemed really angry.

Beckton looked at us both, then nodded to his secretary. "It's OK, Betty, I'll deal with it."

"Ah," I said, "I thought it was you I saw coming in a few minutes ago. So you're going to Belfast a little later, are you?"

He sat back in his chair, and his mouth twisted in a wry expression, neither angry nor embarrassed.

"Let's cut the crap, shall we, Mr. McCausland? You and I know that I just didn't want to see you."

I sat down, uninvited, on the chair in front of the desk.

"Yes, that's obvious. But I'm just wondering why exactly..."

"Can't you work that out? I don't know what it is precisely you're after, in your search for material on the 30s, but it's not something I feel I want to help you with."

I waited for him to say more, but he just sat there, fixing me with his grey eyes. I noted that he wasn't wearing his heavy-framed glasses this morning. They lay neatly folded on one corner of his desk. Perhaps he only put them on, I thought, for effect.

"And why don't you want to help me, in particular?"

He leaned forward, and reached for the glasses. Instead of putting them on he just held them in one hand in front of him, waving them vaguely as he spoke.

"Mr. McCausland, let's not be naive. There are dozens of people nowadays doing what they call 'research' into the past of this unhappy province. And most of them don't have the best of motives. Most of them are intent on raking up dirt about this public figure or that, or re-writing history...from a nationalist perspective mostly. And as the editor of a newspaper which prides itself on upholding..."

I interrupted him. "But I'm a Protestant. And I've no interest in re-writing history from anyone's perspective."

He gave a low, ironic chuckle. "That's what they all say," he said, leaning back again in his chair.

"But you gave full access to your archives to Ray Conlon."

D.P. Beckton froze.

"How do you know that?" he demanded. He was obviously furious.

"Let's say that Ray and I have been comparing notes."

His smooth, angular jaw was set firm, but you could almost hear the swearwords running through his brain. Then he relaxed a little and said:

"That's a bit different, you'll have to agree. Dr Conlon is an academic, from a respected university in the United States. You have to give access..."

"But he's a Catholic," I said, "and clearly has a nationalist perspective on... re-writing the past."

The look he gave me was as black as any anyone has ever wasted on me.

Then, suddenly, his whole demeanour changed. He raised his arms in a gesture of helplessness and smiled a broad smile.

"Look, forgive me...I thought for a moment that one of my staff must have been telling you things they weren't supposed to. And that made me angry...Would you care for a cup of coffee? Or tea?"

I shook my head. "I still want to know why you let Ray Conlon see your records, while you told me you didn't have any archives."

He got up and moved to the coffee maker which stood on a table near the window.

"Dr Conlon applied to us some time ago," he said, putting in a new filter. "And he gave us specific areas that he wanted to research..."

"Yes, the Brannigan's Mill affair. Which is also very relevant to my own queries."

Beckton shrugged as he spooned coffee into the filter. "But I wasn't to know that, was I? You came here, virtually unannounced, and started asking about some guy I'd never heard of called...what was it? Marty McColl?"

I noticed that his strange accent had reappeared. Yes, there were definite local intonations. But I was now sure, in spite of his protestations, that he had spent some considerable time across the ocean.

"Matty Coyle," I said. I didn't want to admit it, but his explanations were becoming more plausible than I'd expected.

"Whatever," he went on. "And if you look at it from my point of view, as an editor with a tradition to uphold, if I start allowing any Tom, Dick or Harry to root round in my archives, and they then go and start throwing accusations or allegations about, maybe against modern-day personalities...well, there are certain people, in certain parties, who aren't going to be pleased with me...if you catch my drift?"

The coffee pot was now gurgling away merrily, but Beckton had returned to his seat and seemed to have forgotten about it. "I have to admit to you also," he said, and his tone had suddenly become confidential, "that I had an ulterior motive in allowing Ray Conlon to look at our archives."

"You did?" I said, trying not to sound impressed.

"Yes." Once again he leaned forward across the desk. "Where was it you actually met him? Was it by any chance...in the offices of one of our, shall we say, rival publications?"

How could he have known that? I asked myself.

"Well, yes...I suppose it was."

"Aha," said Beckton triumphantly. "I thought as much. You see, I'm intrigued about where our Dr Ray Conlon is coming from. As you say, he's from a nationalist background, and my suspicion is that he wants to, as we've agreed, re-write the history of the troubles in the 1930s. Make this Brannigan's Mill affair the subject of some big new anti-Unionist revelation..."

"So why on earth," I asked coldly, "did you give him access?"

He threw his arms wide. "But don't you see? So I could keep open my lines of communication. So I could win his trust and maybe, just maybe, keep tabs on him."

"Keep tabs on him?"

He remembered the coffee, waiting silently for him in the jar, and went over and poured himself a cup.

"Yes, I've been asking a few people to keep an eye on our friend Conlon. Just to see what sources he intends to use for his so-called 'study', and who he's getting his information from."

I frowned, but couldn't think of any way to answer him. I had to admit his explanation was just about credible. Only just about. But there was something too pat about it, too smooth.

"So," I said, "now that you know more about my motives, you'll have no objections to letting me see your archives..."

He looked at me sharply. But once again relaxed almost at once.

"No, I suppose not...But you probably won't find very much of interest there."

"Why not?"

"Well our mutual friend Ray Conlon said that the 'Constitution's' coverage of the Brannigan Mill affair was rather sparse on detail. Mostly extracts from speeches on the matter by Cyril Beamish, the local Unionist MP. 'Very unsatisfactory' is what Dr. Conlon called it...Virtually no mention of Matty Coyle."

I thought about this. "I wonder why," I said. "After all, the Unionists had an interest in putting their gloss on the affair, just as much as the Nationalists."

Beckton shrugged. "Perhaps they thought the best way of doing that was to give full rein to Beamish. From what I know of the whole thing, the incumbent Unionist was having difficulty fighting off the more extreme people on his own side, so he needed all the press coverage he could get. Obviously my predecessor of that time gave it to him...Sure you won't have a coffee?"

I shook my head.

16.

I did take the chance to look at the 'Constitution' archive, however. Ray Conlon had been right. The paper's coverage of the Brannigan Mill affair was largely a compilation of Cyril Beamish statements and speeches. And they amounted to little more than the constant repetition of the same vaguely worded accusation: that Beamish's motives for wanting to build a factory in that particular spot were purely political: to alter the balance of the population in that part of mid-Derry.

I left the newspaper's offices after barely an hour and walked back along the embankment pondering what I had found out that morning. The first question was: did I believe what Beckton had told me about keeping tabs on Ray Conlon? There was something decidedly inconsistent about his version of events. He had helped Conlon, but said he was really keeping a watch on him. He had refused to help me, and was now pretending we were really on the same side. I wasn't sure I bought it.

I wandered up the busy main street, past the clock tower. There were a couple of decent bookshops in the town, and I thought I might browse in their local history sections to see if I could pick up anything there.

But my search was fruitless. Local historians obviously thought it was wiser, in popular editions anyway, to brush over the outbreaks of communal strife which had blighted the past.

I decided to call it a day and head back to the farm. I had parked my car outside a supermarket only a couple of blocks from the newspaper office. So my path led me back along the embankment in that direction.

The Constitution was situated on the corner of the river embankment and a narrow side street leading towards the supermarket. I had already turned into the busy side street, crowded with shoppers and lined by parked cars, and was maybe fifty yards past the paper's main entrance when for no particular reason I glanced back. And stopped in my tracks.

Several people had just come out of the 'Constitution's' entrance and were standing on the pavement in animated conversation. I recognised one of them at once. It was Ray Conlon.

There were two others, and when one of them turned for a moment I saw that it was Beckton himself. The third was someone I didn't immediately recognise. He was taller than average, with an athletic frame, and was wearing an outmoded felt hat. As I stood dithering on the pavement a woman almost barged into me with her baby in a buggy. I apologised profusely, and when I looked up I saw that the three men had parted. Conlon and Beckton had begun walking away from me towards the embankment, while the third man had turned and was walking quickly in my direction along the other side of the street.

I had to make a snap decision. Should I follow Beckton and Conlon and see where they were off to so cosily together? Might it not be amusing to catch up with them and pop a few awkward questions? My instinct told me at once it would be a waste of time. By confronting them I might only force them to clam up. I'd get more out of each of them if they were not together.

My attention switched to the third man, the one coming towards me. He had reached a point almost opposite, across the narrow street, and was glancing both ways, preparing to cross. It was only then that I realised who he was.

It was Hill, the man who had threatened Shenagh Kelly! And had subsequently accosted me outside Francorelli's.

He was bound to recognise me if he saw me. I turned away and looked in a shop window. Hi-fi equipment and electrical goods. I stared dumbly at a portable radio for at least thirty seconds. Then I looked round, half afraid he might be there, right behind me. But he had walked past, and I caught sight of him some way along the street, just as he turned into the supermarket car park.

A very strange meeting indeed! I thought. What was it, I wondered, that had brought together an Irish American academic, a Unionist newspaperman and a Republican hard man? Or was it perhaps true that Hill wasn't that at all, but a security agent? Even so, what could his links be with Ray Conlon?

I didn't really want to follow Hill into the car park. My instinct was to head quickly in the opposite direction. But Beckton and Conlon had long disappeared along the embankment, and it was pointless now to follow them. Slowly I turned back towards my car.

Was there part of me, all the same, that wanted to follow Sean Hill, just out of curiosity? The idea certainly crossed my mind, and it tickled some inborn craving for excitement and mystery. But as I reached the car park I dismissed it as crazy. In this place it was dangerous to indulge such fantasies. Who knows who the man might be, and how he might react if he suspected he was being followed?

So I paused before going on and looked all round the darkening car park. Hill was nowhere to be seen. Perhaps he'd had his car parked here and had already left? Or had walked across the cark park and gone on somewhere else. I pulled my anorak collar closer round my face, hoping that if I did stumble across him he wouldn't recognise me.

I got into my car, started the engine and headed for the exit.

And then suddenly a car pulled out right in front of me. It was a sleek but outmoded racer, possibly dark green, similar to the one I'd seen Hill get into back in Derry.

The driver's face had been a blur. But was it just my imagination, or had his eyes rested on me for just a few seconds before he pulled out?

Had he been waiting for me?

Was he now challenging me: go ahead, follow me if you want?

If it was indeed Hill, I knew he would probably be heading back towards Derry. That was the way I was going too, though I would turn off at Limavady to go back to Bob's farm. So there was nothing I could do for the first few miles anyway but follow the man in the green car.

I tried to dawdle at traffic lights and zebra crossings. At one crossing, just before the Bann bridge, I slowed down and stopped for two indolent teenagers to cross, even though they were still five yards away. Two angry hoots from behind. I waited for the youthful pair to cross, then turned on to the bridge and over it. Alas, the green car was still only a couple of hundred yards ahead of me. And by the next set of traffic lights I was right behind him again.

The evening had begun to draw in, and I comforted myself with the thought that in half an hour or so it would be quite dark. It would be difficult to follow the car in front even if I wanted to. And now one of the impatient cars behind me had overtaken noisily and was between me and my unwanted quarry.

By the time we were leaving the outskirts of Coleraine I'd stopped worrying. There were at least two cars between me and the green coup— and the cars in front were picking up speed on the dual carriageway. I could relax and think about other things.

I thought back to the conversation I had just witnessed outside the newspaper office, and why Hill should be meeting Beckton and Conlon. There must be some quite simple explanation, I decided. Conlon, probably, had returned to Coleraine to do more research at the 'Constitution' and Dougherty's man Hill had taken him there, as a courtesy. Perfectly natural. Nothing strange at all...

I suddenly realised that the cars between me and the green car had both turned off into housing estates on the outskirts of the town. I was now directly behind him again. We were approaching a major roundabout and the road was brilliantly lit by street lighting. No way of hiding. I glanced in the rear view mirror. No one behind me.

I slowed for the roundabout, more than I would normally have done. But he seemed to go even more slowly. I thought of turning off on to one of the side roads, just to get away from the green car in front, but decided that would be pushing things a bit too far. I would simply hang back after the roundabout, where the road rose over the mountains, and allow him to pull away.

But the slower I drove, the slower he drove too. We were now past the roundabout and heading into open country, but he wasn't picking up speed at all. I was no more than thirty or forty yards behind him. There was no longer any street lighting, and the road was in virtual darkness apart from the two sets of headlights. I could read his number-plate clearly. Yes, Derry city. And I could see his head silhouetted against his own headlights.

Was he playing with me? Was he the sort who was used to such situations, and knew how to deal with them?

I would have to pass him. Maybe that was what he wanted, so that he could follow me? But the road was increasingly dark and also twisty. And when I accelerated and came close to the car in front, he seemed to accelerate too, and edge out to discourage me from passing.

This was getting past a joke. I thought of stopping altogether. But there was no lay-by, and in any case, to stop would have been the most suspicious thing of all to do—virtually an admission that I had been following him. So I held on grimly, driving at an unnaturally slow pace on the dark country road, alone with the enemy.

The road rose slowly into the wooded hill country that divides the valleys of the Bann and the Roe. It was lonely, sparsely inhabited country, and I found myself becoming more and more nervous.

But the road here had been improved. There were now long, straight stretches, and since it was completely dark you could see oncoming cars from miles away. We rounded a long, gentle curve and I suddenly saw my chance. A straight, empty road for at least half a mile. I pressed down the accelerator and surged forward to overtake the car ahead of me.

I swept past easily and kept my foot on the accelerator as I shot along the straight towards the next bend. In the rear view mirror I saw his headlights rapidly recede, and by the time I slowed for the next corner he was several hundred yards behind me.

I didn't cut my speed, however, until I was well down into the valley, nearing the outskirts of Limavady.

The last red glow of the sun was dying on the western horizon, clinging to the woods and hills and houses around me as if reluctant to lose them to the night. Columns of smoke rose from some cottages to my right, straight into the windless sky, their greyness tinged with crimson.

When I reached the turn-off to Dungiven there was no sign of any car behind me. I heaved a huge sigh of relief at the thought that I'd given him the slip.

17.

My fuel gauge was reading low, just touching the red band above the empty mark. I probably had enough to get me back to the farm, but the last filling station before my destination was here, just as you left Limavady. Best to stop and fill her up.

At the petrol station I bought the latest issue of both the Derry Reporter and the Foyle Herald. In the latter I caught a glimpse, as I paid for my fuel, of a familiar face. I paused before I went back to the car and took a closer look.

'US ACADEMIC RETURNS TO CLEAR UP MURDER MYSTERY', read the caption.

"Dr Rafael Conlon, of St Daniel's College Baltimore, USA,' the story ran, 'is currently in County Derry conducting research into the industrial and sectarian unrest of the 1930s in the North of Ireland. The focus of his attention at the moment is the affair of Brannigan's shirt mill at Upperfields, near Ballymully. 'One thing that particularly interests me,' Dr Conlon told the Herald, 'is the fate of a central player in that affair, a young schoolteacher called Matthew Coyle.' Some sixty years ago Mr Coyle was a leader of the Upperfields Defence Association, campaigning for equal rights in employment. But on February 8th 1936 he was found drowned in mysterious circumstances in a mill pond in Banagher Glen, between Limavady and Ballymully. 'I didn't know too much about Matty Coyle before I came here,' Dr Conlon told us. 'But the more I look into this affair, the more I'm convinced of one thing: if we establish once and for all the identity of those responsible for Matty Coyle's death, the more we will understand the true reasons why Brannigan's factory was closed down before it was even built. His death has never adequately been explained, and I guess it's now become an ambition of mine to follow this through and clear up a killing which has been left uninvestigated for far too long'. . ."

I stalked back to my car and threw the newspaper on the passenger seat in disgust. What was Conlon playing at? How dare he pretend it was he who was trying to clear up the mystery of Matty's death? I felt a sudden irrational possessiveness over the case. Matty was my relative, not his! Had Conlon suddenly realised he might be able to use anything I found out about Matty to bolster his own findings—and tailor them to fit his own Nationalist-inspired theories? Yes, and maybe, as he saw it, boost his academic prestige as well?

Or had he some other end in sight? Whatever his motives, it seemed he had not been altogether honest in his remarks to the local press.

I slammed the car into first gear and raced across the station forecourt, almost knocking over a man in blue overalls. He shouted something angrily, but I merely waved and drove out on to the road.

Come on! I said to myself, calm down. So Conlon has stolen your lines! But maybe that's a good thing. After all, he has more experience of this sort of thing. Maybe he'll get further than you. He certainly has better contacts on the Nationalist side! And then he'd be obliged to share what he found. It just underlines that he and you have an obvious interest in working together...

But in spite of myself I couldn't help feeling that Conlon and I were now rivals, competing to find out the truth about Matty Coyle. And present it with a particular gloss.

The roads were now narrower and more twisted, and I ambled along casually, glad I would soon be home, tucking into a good farmhouse meal. A couple of cars overtook and passed me. I was aware of a third approaching fast. He came right up behind me, but seemed to hesitate before passing.

We turned into a long straight, and I slowed even further, turning on my left-hand indicator as a sign to him to pass. Still he seemed to hesitate. Then suddenly he swerved out and accelerated past me.

It was a dark green coupe.

He drove ahead until there was a gap of a hundred yards or so, then slowed down. I was in exactly the same position as before, on the main road from Coleraine. If I didn't drive really slowly I would again be right behind him, on his tail. And that that was the last thing I really wanted.

The only comforting side of the situation was that we had almost reached the turn-off for Banagher. He wouldn't know I intended to turn off. He would presumably go on towards Ballymully. And I would swing suddenly into the side road, and lose him.

But to my astonishment and alarm, as we rounded the bend before the turn-off the green car started to signal to turn right, the same way I was going. He slowed down as we approached the intersection, his right-hand indicator winking, until I was almost up with him. Only then did he begin to turn into the side-road. He knew where I was living! And he was taunting me.

I took a quick decision. Instead of following him to the right I put my foot on the accelerator and sped off down the road towards Ballymully, as fast as I could.

After half a mile I stopped in a lay-by, to give me time to think. However incredible it seemed, Hill must have recognised me in Coleraine. And he obviously knew where I was staying. So he hadn't worried about losing me on the main road. He knew he would pick me up nearer home. And...and then what? Follow me to the farm? Waylay me on the quiet, deserted road that led there?

Or was I just over-reacting? There was no real reason, I told myself, for Sean

Hill to be interested in me. He knew who I was, it was true. At least, he knew that I was looking into the events of 1935 in Upperfields. So what was sinister about that? Ray Conlon was doing much the same research, and he seemed to be well in with Hill's boss, Joe Dougherty—presuming, that is, that comrade Sean was indeed working for Dougherty…

Perhaps Hill had recognised me back at Coleraine, and decided to have a little fun—allowing me to catch up with his car, then pretending to follow me…

But that wouldn't explain how he had found me again, on the road between here and Limavady. And then I also remembered what Hill had said to Lottie's niece Shenagh, back in the Bogside. "Tell McCloskey to clear off and not come calling again…If it comes to my ears that he and this other geezer are bothering Lottie…" What had he threatened to do? "Just let them know something very nasty might happen."

And he knew where I was staying!

Or did he? Was it possible that Sean Hill might have taken the road to Banagher for some quite innocuous reason, nothing to do with me or my relatives? I thought for a moment. Where did the road lead? After it passed Young Bob's house it curved to the right to follow the course of Banagher Glen. Then it forked, and one of the forks, I realised, turned down towards the point where the glen opened into the flatlands. And it crossed the river at Upperfields bridge.

That was where he was going!

I felt a huge sense of relief. Of course, that was the explanation. Or if he wasn't going to meet someone in Upperfields, perhaps he was going through it, towards the road which led to Claudy and then back to Derry. It was possible to go that way to Derry. The roads weren't so good, but it was probably shorter than by the main roads.

In any case, if Hill had really been following me, or even playing games with me, he would not have allowed me just to scoot down the road towards Ballymully. He would have turned and followed me, surely. He would have been here by now, parked right behind me in the lay-by!

I started my engine again, and glanced in the mirror.

No, nothing at all behind. At least, nothing that I could see in the pitch darkness of the empty country road.

I turned out and continued towards Ballymully. I had decided to take a different route to the farm, just in case. I would continue a mile or two further along this road, then turn off into another by-road which joined the one Hill had taken only a few hundred yards from the farm.

I found the turn and drove slowly along the narrow, twisting country roads, thinking about the day's events. Even though I knew the green car had not come this way, I half expected as I turned each bend to see it parked by the road, waiting for me. But there was nothing and nobody. I did catch a glimpse of headlights flaring into the darkness somewhere across the dark countryside in front of me, possibly on the direct road to the farm. But it must have been a mile away or more.

I came to the road along which Hill must have passed. At the junction I paused, peering right and left for any sign of a car lying in wait. I had been unnerved by Hill's sudden reappearance behind me on the road from Limavady. But did I really think he could mind read? Or that he had a honing device attached to my car? I knew he couldn't have, because he had not had a chance to put one there...I told myself not to be paranoid!

I pulled out and drove the quarter mile to the end of Young Bob's lane.

Here I paused again.

Curiosity has always been my downfall. And the tempter suddenly stirred in my heart.

"Go and have a look at Upperfields!" he whispered to me. "Go and see if he's parked there! You remember the pub near the bridge...He might be parked there, and then you'll know he has a rendezvous. And you could even go into the pub and find out, maybe, who it is!"

I laughed at myself. No, don't be so daft! You've just heaved an enormous sigh of relief after throwing the enemy off your scent. Why tempt fate by following him into the lion's den?

I sat at the lane end for several minutes, with the engine ticking over gently. Then I released the brake and swung back into the road, heading for Upperfields.

What the heck! It was just a hamlet with a shop, a pub and a row of new council houses. What could possibly happen to me in such a small, quiet place?

18.

The road wound on for about half a mile until it came to a fork. The road to the right led back to Limavady. The one to the left, which I followed, continued straight for half a mile, then turned sharply downhill into a hollow. I could see the glow of lighted buildings somewhere down among the trees. At the bottom of the hill the road plunged into a wood, performed a couple of twists and ran out on to a narrow, slightly humped bridge with rough stone parapets on either side.

As I drove slowly over the hump a building came in view, and a lighted sign. It said: "THREE CORNERS INN".

Why did that name ring a bell? I was sure I had never known the name of the pub in Upperfields. We had never been encouraged, Eric and I, to come to the hamlet. At Banagher farm it was seen as alien territory. But the name "Three Corners Inn" was very fresh in my mind...

Of course! The newspaper article Ray Conlon and I had found in the Foyle Herald offices. This was the very hostelry, then, where Aloysius Brannigan had stood for his photograph, alongside Father Delaney and the other members of the Upperfields Development Association. Including a certain M. Coyle.

Upperfields, in fact, was little more than the Three Corners Inn. There was a row of new council houses beyond the pub, and the lights of a few scattered homes peered dimly through the surrounding trees. And that was it. The road here divided again into two, with the more substantial branch going straight past the inn to the right, up the hill towards Claudy and the Derry road. The other, narrower branch turned left and cut between the pub and the river, heading towards the glen, Banagher lake and the mill house. Across the road from the pub was a broad parking area, and I pulled into one of the few empty spaces, by a parapet overlooking the river.

The Inn turned out to be quite a substantial establishment, more a hotel than just a pub. Its ground floor windows were all brightly lit, though because of the misted glass you could only see vague forms and the occasional movement within. When I switched the engine off I could hear the steady murmur of inebriated voices, punctuated now and then by a raucous cry or hearty laughter.

From the shelter of the car I surveyed the other vehicles parked round me. It wasn't difficult to spot the green coupe. It was parked at the end of the row across the road, just outside the pub. Sean Hill, then, was here, and was meeting someone inside.

I was tempted! Just to go in and see what he was doing, who it was he was meeting. Maybe quietly ask one of the regulars how often he came here and what his business was in Upperfields? But I banished the idea at once. This was probably home territory for Hill. I was the stranger. And I was from the other side of the glen, and that would stand out like a sore thumb.

Still, why not get to know the lie of the land? I opened the car door and got out.

It was a clear night, with a bright, almost full moon high in the sky. Its glow was obscured only sporadically by ragged clouds. The wind had begun to rise, and as I walked back towards the bridge the rushing noise it made in the trees mingled with the gentler, steadier gush of the river below.

I reached the signpost where the road forked. Banagher 1 1/2, read the finger that pointed past the inn. Claudy 8, said the finger pointing up the hill. The moon's reflection shone dully on the smooth surface of the tarmac. I turned right and moved to the brow of the bridge, pausing to look down on the stream. But there was little I could see in the dark space below me. Only the faintest hint of moonlight glinting on the rushing, rippling surface of the water.

Downstream the glen broadened out, and in the dim moonlight I could see open fields sloping gently upwards on either side. Where, I wondered, had the site been for the proposed factory? Someone had told me it was on the right bank of the bridge, on the 'Protestant' side. But there didn't seem to be room in this narrow valley to construct a building of any size. Perhaps it hadn't been here at the bridge at all, but somewhere on the flatter land higher up.

I continued to the far side of the bridge. And here the first thing I noticed was a narrow, dark lane leading off the road, to the left, down towards the river. I decided to explore.

Only a few yards into the darkness and I regretted my decision. The path was uneven, and I tripped on a loose stone and almost lost my balance. A moment later and my face brushed against brambles or thorn branches protruding from the high hedges on either side. I decided to go back.

But as I turned I noticed a patch of relative lightness in the vegetation to one side. The moonlight flowing through it was sufficient to show a low bank, and a gap in the hedgerow. I scrambled up to it, and peered through.

I knew at once I had found the site of Brannigan's factory. It was a sloping field, so wide that even in the bright moonlight I couldn't see any fence or hedge at the far side. But at some time or other there had been excavation here. A roughly rectangular shape had been cut in the hillside, evidently to accommodate a building, and the debris from the cut had been levelled to form a platform above the river.

I was filled with a strange emotion. It was as if I was looking into history, and the gap in the hedge was a window specially designed for my enlightenment.

The ghostly light of the moon threw strange and inexplicable shadows over the hollows and hillocks of the ground before me, and as I stood staring at the empty field my mind began to play tricks. I imagined not only a gaunt, red-brick building taking shape above the river but also tiny figures, like ants, scurrying in and out of the half-completed factory…

"Yes," said a voice, frighteningly loud, from behind me. "This is where the factory should have been."

I turned sharply, but could see nothing in the dark. Only a vague movement, as if someone was edging towards me down the path.

I said nothing, waiting for the man to speak again. His voice, strong and confident, had a strangely frivolous tone to it, jocular but also mocking.

"A strange time of day to come exploring," he said. "I assure you it's easier to see in the daytime."

I was confused. This wasn't Hill's dark monotone. The voice was lighter, the accent clearer. But I knew who it was. It was Joe Dougherty, the republican councillor I had met in Derry. At the newspaper office. The one with the southern accent.

"I was just on my way home," I said, trying to make light of my strange behaviour. "My relatives live just a mile or two from here. And I decided to come and look at the famous metropolis of Upperfields."

Somehow I had fallen into the same easy, bantering tone that Dougherty himself was fond of. He moved closer, and I tried to make out whether he was alone or not. He was still standing in the dark, though he was only a few paces from me. For some time there was silence. Then he spoke again.

"They'd even begun to build, over there in the far corner. If you look carefully you can just see a few low walls. But then all work was suspended…And no one ever bothered to demolish the walls they'd already built."

"Why did they stop?" I asked, turning back towards the ghostly, moonlit site. I wasn't at all sure I could see the walls he was referring to.

"After Matty Coyle died Brannigan began to have second thoughts. It was the Depression, you see, and his business interests back in the States weren't going so well…I believe he died a few years later, bankrupt and a broken man."

"A sad end for someone who…well, I suppose meant well."

"Meant well?" Dougherty chuckled. Then there was another pause. "Brannigan was simply supporting his own people. As he was bound to do. Don't you see that?"

I glanced towards him, but in the darkness I couldn't even make out his face, let alone his expression. A harshness had come into his voice, however, that had not been there before.

"And if everyone just went on…blindly supporting their own side, that would solve something?" I asked.

I sensed, rather than saw, him stir in the darkness. "Yes," he said emphatically. "Sooner or later one side is bound to give way, and then there's always a solution."

"And you're absolutely certain, aren't you, which side that's going to be!"

"Of course!" he said, and the frivolous note had suddenly come back into his voice. "Our day will certainly come…"

He gave a short laugh.

"But let's not be so serious. Come on and have a drink in the bar. Perhaps I could introduce you to some of the people who are going to make it all happen?"

I gave a snort of amusement, in spite of myself.

"That's very kind of you," I said, "but I'm not so sure they'd be very glad to meet me."

"Why not?" he said with feigned surprise. "It's said you should always get to know your enemy…and these poor guys have probably never had the chance!"

"Why are you so sure that I'm their enemy?"

Instead of a reply he climbed up and joined me on the bank. Now I saw his face showing dimly in the pallid light of the moon.

"You see those lights over there?" he asked, nodding towards the dark countryside beyond the field. A light drizzle had begun to fall, making it even more difficult to see anything. I could just about make out a dull orange glow, probably some miles distant, which I hadn't noticed before.

"That's what we call the 'stockade'," he said. "I believe the owner himself calls it 'Shangri La'…" He laughed ironically. "But it's surrounded by wire and floodlights, and he has guard dogs and even armed men in there, so that he can sleep at night…"

"It's not where Mervyn Ritchie lives, is it?" I suggested.

He nodded.

"Now you see, Mr McCausland, as far as I'm concerned you have to be either inside that stockade looking out…or outside it, looking in. That's the situation we're in, whether you like it or not…"

"I disagree," I said, cutting him short. "People who live next to each other don't have to be enemies, just because they think differently."

"Think differently? I think there's a bit more to it than that." Again he gave a chuckle. "The problem is, surely, that they want to live in different countries."

I stepped down off the bank and looked up at his silhouette.

"Yes, but that shouldn't be a reason for killing each other," I said. "We have to start accepting each other for what we are, try to understand each other. And then try to work out some solution."

There was another brief silence. "We've never had any difficulty in accepting what the unionists are," he said. And this time there was no irony in his voice.

I sighed. "I'd be glad to meet you for a drink," I said. "But some other time. It's a bit late in the day and I'm just a bit tired. Anyway, if we went on talking like this we might create more misunderstandings than we would resolve..."

The light was just strong enough for me to see his shadowy figure nod.

"You know, I think you're probably right," he said. "About creating misunderstandings, that is. And I agree, we should meet again. It's been quite a revelation, Mr McCausland." And he hopped down off the bank as well. Then he seemed just to melt into the darkness. I guessed rather than saw that he was walking back up the path towards the road.

I followed, though after a while I could no longer hear any sound in front of me, and I thought he had vanished as noiselessly as he had come. But I found he was waiting for me at the end of the bridge. We walked across together as far as the fingerpost.

"I'll be in touch then," he said cheerfully. "You're staying at your cousin's farm, I take it?"

"Actually I think I'll probably move out tomorrow. Life with the relatives isn't always easy...They're good people, but there's a limit even to their hospitality."

"So where will you move to?"

"I haven't decided yet."

"You could move here," he said, nodding towards the Three Corners Inn. And with another low laugh he slipped off towards the pub entrance. He made no offer to shake my hand.

"My relatives will know where I am," I called after him.

"Don't worry," he replied, "I'll find you, wherever you are."

That was the second time I'd been told that in little more than twenty-four hours.

19.

"Is he still annoyed with me, Milly?" I asked when I got back to the farm. Young Bob had already gone to bed, but Milly had stayed up specially to give me my supper.

"Oh don't take any notice of him, Adrian," she said. "He'll sulk for two days and then be as right as rain...We all know you're right, in the long run, that the Bible tells us to be good neighbours to everyone. And we have no problem with people like the Devlins next door. Or with Michael Fallon and his family...But there are some of them ones that just don't want to be good neighbours to us, and it's difficult to be friendly with people like that, if you see what I mean."

I nodded. "I do, Milly, I do...but then the other side could say much the same about some of our people."

She let out a cackle. "Aye, I was just saying to Beth Thompson yesterday, the Devlins are having trouble again with that Herbie Wallace fellow, awful curmudgeon that he is. He's claiming some of the land in the hollow between the farms, that's always been the Devlins' as far as we know...And, well, it's not difficult to know which side we're on."

She poured me another cup of tea.

"By the way, there was a man after you earlier, on the phone. Said it was urgent. He would be awake until midnight, he said, on that number..."

She gave me his name and number. It was Ray Conlon.

"Hi there," he said when I phoned. "Sorry to disturb you so late. I wanted to fix a meeting with you, as soon as possible."

"Okay," I said, a little reluctantly. I was still annoyed about his newspaper interview. And perplexed by his strange meeting in Coleraine. "Are you still at your house near Dungiven?"

"That's the point. I'll be away for a day or two. I'm heading south tomorrow. But coming back in a couple of days. Could we meet at Upperfields, maybe? At the famous Three Corners Inn, where the Defence Association used to have its meetings?"

"Er no," I said sharply. "If it's all the same to you I'd prefer to meet somewhere else..."

He seemed a bit put out. "But they do good basket lunches there..."

"No, I really don't want to meet in that particular place."

"Sure, if you say so. You must have your reasons...How about meeting, then, where we met before? Down at the mill in Banagher glen..."

"Fine, what do you want to talk about?"

"I've found something. I mean, something of real interest. It definitely connects your father to Matty Coyle."

"Well, I know that my father was connected to Matty," I said a little shortly. "What I don't know is how they were both involved in the Upperfields affair, and what connection my father had to Matty's death."

"Yes, I think what I've found throws some light on all of that."

"You do? So what is it you've found then?"

"A document."

"A document?" I said, thinking of the obituary I had found in the library. "Not a newspaper cutting, by any chance?"

"No," he answered, obviously puzzled. "It's a letter..."

Another nasty suspicion crossed my mind.

"You didn't get it from Lottie Coyle, by any chance?"

"How did you...?" He stopped, and was silent for a moment. "You've been to Lottie's too..."

"Yes," I said, "and she certainly didn't tell me anything interesting. Perhaps you told her she shouldn't say anything if a mysterious stranger came visiting...?"

"Look, I'm trying to help you here. I'm offering to share the one bit of information I got out of her."

I knew I had gone too far. "OK, I'm sorry," I said. "It's just that she told me absolutely nothing, and yet I had a strong feeling she knew more than she was saying...She's been leaned on by someone."

"Not by me," he said firmly. So firmly, indeed, that I believed him.

"Okay, what's this letter you got from her?"

"I don't want to discuss it over the phone. As I say, I'm coming back the day after tomorrow. Can you meet me at the watermill that day?"

"I'm afraid that won't be possible. I'm out of County Derry myself for a couple of days. How about Friday?"

"Friday?" He sounded a bit anxious, as if it might not wait until then. "Well, okay, if that's the earliest you can make it...My time over here is running out. I have to get back to the States early next week..."

"Yes, I've taken unpaid leave too...time presses, I know."

He sighed. "But that's what makes life worth living, isn't it?"

"How do you mean?" I asked.

"If we had endless time on our hands life would be so boring...and pointless. What is it they say? It's only because life is so limited, and the clock is always ticking down on us, that each hour of it becomes so precious..."

"Scarcity certainly adds value to any commodity," I agreed.

He gave a short laugh.

"Enough philosophy!" he said. "What shall we say then? Friday morning around eleven? At the tea house by the mill, where we met before?"

"Okay, it will be closed of course. The season's ended. But that will make it all the better. We won't be disturbed...And, Dr Conlon, I'd just like to say..."

"Please call me Ray..."

"Okay, Ray...I apologise for the snide comments just now. This thing is getting on my nerves a bit."

"Yeah, I can appreciate that. I'm feeling a bit edgy myself...Until Friday then."

20.

The next day, after I'd booked into a motel near Limavady, I drove to Derry. There I joined Tim McCloskey and we set off together to Mayo. Tim had located Father Maurice O'Sullivan, the priest quoted in the *Western Argus* as Father Delaney's 'friend and colleague'. And he'd also offered to drive me there.

"This thing's getting interesting!" he said. "I want to know what happens next."

The stretch of country between Derry and Mayo is among the most beautiful in Ireland. The Bluestack mountains, Donegal Bay, and the mountains of Sligo, which culminate in the great wedge-shaped rampart of Ben Bulben pointing defiantly out towards the ocean and the ceaseless west winds...But I was in no mood to enjoy scenery. I hadn't slept much the night before and I dozed for much of the way.

The car gave a sudden jolt and I sat bolt upright, looking about me in confusion.

The scene around us seemed unreal. The car had just passed over a cattle grid and was now half-way along a promontory jutting into the sea. Sheer hundred-foot cliffs dropped away beneath us on either side. I could see the water seething restlessly among the dark teeth of the rocks below. I looked up from the frothing water and there ahead, where the promontory opened out, stood a gaunt grey building. We were approaching it rapidly, rising up from the thin causeway of rock which connected it to the mainland. I wondered if St. Francis's had consciously been located at this point to symbolise the dividing line between certainty and doubt, the last frontier between solid dry land and the leap of faith which took people out on to the stormy seas, on their way to another, possibly better, land...

But the building itself was a bit of a monstrosity, set under an untidy jumble of dark neo-gothic roofs, with a crenellated tower at one end and an ornate chapel at the other. Tim parked his car on the wind-swept gravel space in front of the entrance. The main door proved to be a vast varnished affair under a vaulted arch. It opened as we crunched across the gravel, and a small man in clerical garb and glasses emerged to greet us.

Father O'Sullivan would meet us in his own rooms, he told us. Would we like a cup of tea? To be brutally honest I'd been hoping for a bit more. We hadn't eaten anything since that morning except a hamburger at a road-side cafe. And that had been several hours ago, while we were still in County Sligo. I was ravenous, but was too polite to ask openly for food.

We passed swiftly along several cold, high corridors, the noise of our foot-steps magnified by the place's emptiness. All the time I was conscious of the sound of the sea. It must be inescapable here, I thought. I wondered how, if I had been a permanent resident here, I would have reacted after a while to that restless, never-ending presence. I concluded it might well have sent me mad.

Now we began to climb a series of stone staircases, until we came to a sur-prisingly plush landing, with varnished wooden floors and a strip of thick red carpet down the middle. This led to a paneled door, on which our bespectacled guide gently knocked. A gruff yes told us to enter. And we were in the presence of Father O'Sullivan.

Like the promontory on which the building was built, this room had three sides facing out to the sea. I wondered what inner need drove a man to seek such exposure to the elements, especially here, where they were so often inclement. I looked with added interest at the man in black sitting at his ornately carved desk across the room.

The small brother withdrew, closing the door behind him, and the man behind the desk beckoned to us to advance. He made no move to come and meet us, but indicated two cushioned chairs in front of him.

"You've come a long way. I hope it will be worth your while," he said when we were seated. He had a gruff, matter-of-fact voice. Father O'Sullivan was prob-ably over seventy, but he had a vigorous, organised way about him. His face was lean, with lips that kept pursing themselves in a pensive way, and bright grey eyes that watched you warily through square, rimless glasses. He reminded me strongly of photographs I had seen of Eamon de Valera, the first president of the Irish Republic.

"As I explained on the phone, Father," Tim began tentatively, "we were led to believe that you were acquainted with Father Teddy Delaney. And that you were one of the people who knew him best…"

"Yes, I knew him in his final years," said the elderly priest non-committally, and waited for Tim to go on.

"And as I understand, you would know all there is to know about the book he was preparing to write…about the affair at Upperfields in the thirties. That's what I understood you to say on the phone…"

Father O'Sullivan rose abruptly to his feet. "I was forgetting my manners. You'll both have a glass of sherry, won't you?"

Sherry was never quite my drink, but it would have been surly to refuse this courtesy. The priest went to a glass cabinet across the room from his desk and took out a decanter and three glasses. As I sipped the bitter sweet brown liquid, it certainly had the effect of relaxing the muscles round my neck, tense after the long drive.

Our host, meanwhile, had opened a drawer in his desk and pulled out a pipe and a tin of tobacco. "Mind if I smoke?" he asked, directing his question at me. I told him I had no objection.

"The first thing I want to get straight," he said, "is why you're interested in all this." He was talking to me, as if Tim was not even in the room.

I cleared my throat. "Well, it's a slightly complicated story," I said, leaning forward and preparing to explain.

"I have all evening," he said. "The brothers don't expect me to attend all the offices..."

So I outlined briefly the story of my father's exercise books, the single cryptic reference to Matty Coyle, and my fears as to what it meant. I thought that by being as open about it as possible I had the best chance of gaining his confidence. I had the impression he already knew exactly who I was.

Every now and again, as I was telling my story, he would take the pipe out of his mouth and say "mhm" or "aha". At one point, when I mentioned my meeting with Ray Conlon, he immediately stopped chewing on his extinguished pipe and sat up, as if to say something. But after a moment's thought he sat back in his chair again. And when I had finished he just sat there, moving the pipe about in his mouth. He had lit it several times, and each time it had gone out again without his appearing to notice.

Finally he put he pipe down and looked at me. "You say Matty Coyle was related to you?" he asked.

"A distant relative...a second cousin, I think. But yes, definitely a relative."

Father O'Sullivan turned to Tim. "And you, Mr. McCloskey, what's your interest in all this?"

Tim splayed his hands out innocently and beamed at the priest. "I'm just a friend of the family, you know. Lottie Coyle, Matty's sister, lives in my ward in the Bogside..."

Father O'Sullivan's head moved just a fraction, just enough to betray that the mention of Lottie had surprised him. "Matty Coyle's sister is still alive?" he asked.

Tim nodded. "She's getting on a bit now, in her eighties. And she's...a bit lost in her memories, if you know what I mean. But she's alive, yes, very much so."

Father O'Sullivan sat up in his chair and joined his hands on the desk in front of him. "Well, *there's* an interesting thing...So I take it, Mr. McCausland, you'll have already been talking to her, this sister of Matty's, about those days in Upperfields?"

"Oh well, these days Lottie has..." Tim began, but I butted in.

"Lottie's memories are a bit hazy, and what she's told me so far was a bit confused. But yes, I'm hoping she'll still be able to give me some valuable insights into what happened."

Father O'Sullivan looked troubled, but finally he nodded. "Maybe she will, maybe she will...But you'll have realised, won't you, from meeting her...that Lottie is probably not the most reliable of witnesses?"

Now it was my turn to show surprise. Father O'Sullivan seemed astonishingly well informed about Lottie. Even though a moment ago he'd expressed surprise that she was still living.

"Why do you say that?" I asked, frowning.

"Because she was institutionalised...sent to a special school. When she was still quite young, I believe. She was not quite...how shall I put it? Not quite all there."

I gave him what I hoped was a searching look. "You seem very well acquainted with Lottie and her life history."

He smiled affably. "Well, you see, I have a sort of personal interest in the whole thing too. My family are also from near Dungiven. Up near Feeney, actually. That's why Father Delaney and I got on so well and got to know each other when he came to live here in his retirement. We used to talk about that area a lot...And about the Brannigan business in particular. It was, I suppose, his final ambition to complete his account of events and have it published before he departed this life."

"So you talked about his memoirs a lot?" I asked.

"Oh yes, very often. He'd been writing it for several years even before he came here. Thought it would be his contribution to the history of his birthplace. But..."

We waited for him to go on. "But...?" I prompted him.

"Towards the end, when his mind began to wander, you know...he found it difficult to concentrate."

"So did he ever finish it?"

Father O'Sullivan looked down at his desk and started rolling a pencil backward and forward across its polished surface.

"No," he said finally, "he never completed it."

We were all silent for a few moments, as if in tribute to the worthy priest who had never quite reached his life's final target.

"You know, don't you," said Father O'Sullivan abruptly, as if on impulse, "that Lottie was sent here, to Mayo?"

Tim and I looked at each other blankly.

"The institution where she was sent was St. Brigid's." He turned to the window and indicated a distant headland some way along the coast to the west. You could just about make out a whitewashed building there, overlooking the sea. "It was called an orphanage, but I suppose you could call it more accurately a correctional school. The nuns were very strict and were supposed to be able to do wonders with perverse...and stubborn..."

He stopped in mid-sentence, staring vaguely out at the jagged coastline.

"But I thought," I said quietly, "that Lottie was sent here because she was mentally handicapped. Is that...not quite the full truth?"

Father O'Sullivan turned away from the window, but instead of looking at me appeared to rest his eyes on one of the gloomy portraits of ancient prelates hanging on the study wall.

"Oh, they dealt with all sorts," he said with an absent sort of air. "In those days they didn't distinguish much between mental illness and bad behaviour. It was all the work of the devil, wasn't it? The fruits of sin."

There was only a very faint trace of irony in his voice.

"And...what form did Lottie's 'bad behaviour' take?" I asked.

He shrugged. "Who knows?" he said. "In those days it was enough to answer back a teacher in class. Or be seen looking at a boy..."

"How old was she when she was sent here?"

He looked at me as if this question was both surprising and annoying.

"I think she was seventeen or eighteen," he said with some reluctance.

"Hm," was all I said, but I was thinking that at that age it would be quite natural for Lottie to be looking at boys.

There was a short silence. Finally I said: "You say Father Delaney never completed his account of the Upperfields affair. But he did begin it, didn't he, and he even had part of it published in the local newspaper here?"

"Oh yes," our host replied, "he published three instalments in all. And I can give you a copy of those, if you like. But I don't think you'll find much of interest in them. They're mostly a rather rambling account of his life history up to his arrival in Upperfields, and then a description of the place itself...They, er, don't include anything about the dispute itself, or the people involved. But you're welcome to have copies."

He opened a drawer in his desk and pulled out a number of sheets of paper. He placed them carefully on the desktop and I went over and took them. They were photocopies of newspaper articles dating from the 1970s. Father O'Sullivan, it seemed, had had them ready and waiting.

I glanced through them. They would certainly be of some interest, however little they revealed. But I had a strong feeling that Father O'Sullivan was not being entirely honest with me. I looked at him pointedly.

"And that's all you have?" I asked. "What happened to his original manuscript?"

He didn't reply straight away. He had begun rolling the pencil again, back and forth across the table. It was beginning to irritate me.

"I don't know, Mr. McCausland," he said, "whether you have any beliefs, in Christianity or anything else. But could I ask you what you consider the most important quality a human being can have?"

The question took me aback.

"I...well, I suppose," I stammered, desperately trying to think of something sensible to say. "I suppose, well...compassion, maybe?"

He smiled.

Then he got up, slowly and stiffly, and went over to a small door near the one by which we had entered. It opened on to a tiny box-like room, with some sort of cabinet files to one side. Through the door I could see him hesitate, but then he pulled a bunch of keys out of his pocket. A moment later he re-emerged, carrying what looked like a cardboard shoebox.

"I also have this," he said, handing it to me.

It was one of those moments when, for just a few seconds, you don't realise the significance of what has just happened. It was a plain cardboard box, a bit broader, perhaps, than a normal shoebox. Suddenly I realised this might be a sort of breakthrough, the most important moment yet in my search for the truth about Matty Coyle.

I unloosed the string which was tied round the box, and took off the lid.

Underneath lay a thick wadge of type-written pages, placed caringly in clear, light wrapping paper.

"These are the bits which he wrote but never got round to putting in order, so that the *Western Argus* didn't want to publish them. I've been through them a few times, but quite frankly they're so jumbled and incomplete that I couldn't do anything with them. But you may find something there that interests you..."

I felt a sudden thrill of excitement and gratitude. "You mean I can...?"

"You can take them," he said. "I don't suppose I'll ever do anything with them now. And Teddy Delaney would be grateful, I'm sure, that somebody was taking an interest in his story..."

I stood staring down at the manuscript. Then I turned back to Father O'Sullivan.

"You had another visitor in the last day or two, didn't you?" I asked. "An American called Ray Conlon."

He gave me a solemn look, wondering no doubt how I knew, then nodded.

"Why didn't you give this to him?" I said.

The glimmer of a smile came to his face. "He came here with a man I didn't take to very much..."

"Councillor Joe Dougherty," said Tim with a deep breath.

"No, no, that wasn't his name," said Father O'Sullivan. "I think he may also have come from America..."

I was puzzled. Who could that be? Possibly a friend who came over with him, and hadn't been with him on the two occasions we had met.

"You didn't get his name?" I asked.

"No, sorry. He didn't give a name. Didn't seem very keen to answer when I asked..."

Even more puzzling. But I couldn't think who it might have been, so I let it drop.

I shook Father O'Sullivan's hand warmly. "Thank you," I said with feeling. "I'm very grateful to you."

There was a strong smell of cabbage and mutton in the corridor as we left his study, but Father O'Sullivan had not invited us to stay for dinner. Outside it was rapidly growing dark. As we edged cautiously back over the narrow isthmus towards the mainland it was Tim who broke the silence.

"What about a pint or two before we set off home?"

"Yes, let's do that..."

Then, as the lights of first little town came into view, I said:

"On second thoughts, why don't we book into some little hotel? I wouldn't mind staying around for a few hours tomorrow. Make some more inquiries...If you have the time to spare, that is?"

He shrugged. "All the time in the world," he said.

21.

In the hotel in Westport I began reading Fr. Delaney's memoirs. Tim had gone to his room in another part of the hotel quite early, after a couple of pints in the bar. It was a wild evening, with high winds and rain lashing against the window. But I was so wrapped up in what I was reading that I hardly noticed.

"Upperfields was not my first parish,' the text began. *'I had been at Collooney in the County Sligo before, and before that in Kiltimagh in the County Mayo. But it was my first parish in the North. I was being sent there, Bishop McCann said, to use what he called my calming influence. 'You're an emollient man, Fr Delaney,' I remember he said, and I wasn't at all sure at that point what the word meant, 'you're an emollient man, and your peace-keeping instincts will be much in demand round there.'*

Well, I suppose I knew what he was driving at. 'You don't use ten words, Teddy,' my sister Kathleen used to say to me, 'if you can use fifty.' But I always found it was a good way of calming people down. Just talk to them. Don't just talk any rubbish, but talk in a kindly way, and don't let them get a word in edgeways...It's a technique that has served me well down the years."

I smiled, and skipped several paragraphs which seemed to be in the same tenor. Clearly I was going to have to be selective in my reading of the good father's memoirs. Though I had to admit I was warming to him.

I came to a passage which appeared to be more to the point...

"...It was at this stage that a delegation from the parish came to me and said: 'Father, they're starting this Association thing, to argue the case for encouraging Mr Brannigan to build his mill (we had all heard of Brannigan by this time, and he had even visited the townland to scout out a good site for his factory). And we've heard they want to bring in people from Ballymully to join it, and from further up towards Feeney and the Fore Glen. If this mill is to be for the people of Upperfields, we need to get our own people on this committee. And I have to say I agreed with them, though maybe not for the reasons they were thinking. You see, I had heard that some of the people from outside that were trying to get on to the committee were people who were spoiling for a fight. Things were getting tense in those days, all over the North, and some people saw the question of the factory as a perfect way of opening new fronts in the battlefield...

Anyway, these good folks said: We were wondering, Father, if you would agree to join the as-sociation, so as to make sure it's in the interests of local people and that there's no jiggery pokery over the mill...(Why they all insisted on calling it a mill, I do not know. It was to be a textile factory, but somehow the folk all round began to call it 'Brannigan's Mill'. I used to tell them the only mill round here is the ould one down in Banagher Glen, that has not worked for these past twenty years..."

I skipped another massive digression. And my eyes settled on a passage right at the bottom of a page, and two words in that passage in particular.

". . .There was this young fellow, I don't rightly know where he came from, by the name of Matthew Coyle. Or Matty as some people called him."

I took a deep breath and read on.

"Now I have to admit that at first I didn't take much to Matty. Far too clever by half, he was, and always very confident in his own rightness. Not pushy, you understand. Quite the opposite. He would listen for maybe half an hour without saying anything, and then he would slowly, gradually cut in to a conversation, putting these views which—he made clear—he thought nobody could question because, in his view at least, they were so self-evidently right. Also, they say that Matty was quite a charmer with the girls, something that didn't please me too much. . .It was only later, when I saw that the young man had some sense in his head, and was good at explaining himself, that I began to think: this lad could do something for us here, in the community. . ."

"Building the mill was a great idea. And the Association was to a man—there were no women on it, that was the way in those times—to a man they were all for it. But they were split down the middle on the question of whether to approach anyone from the Protestant side about it. Mr Brannigan left it to us. 'You're the people who live there. You decide. I think there should be a few Protestants on your committee, as there should be in the factory too, when it's built. But it's your decision.'

And some said, Mr Brannigan is right. We should ask someone from the Protestant side. Perhaps the rector from Ballymully. But then other people said No. This thing is for Upperfields, and what does the rector of Ballymully know about Upperfields? And others were even more straightforward. They just said: for once there should be a factory for Catholics, and only Catholics. . ."

"It was on an evening in November, I think, that Matty introduced me to a young fellow he said was his friend. I didn't catch his name and I wasn't sure whether he had anything to do with the Association. Sounded as if he had a bit of education, but he seemed a decent enough sort of a lad. I was to find out soon enough who he was, and what role he was to play in the whole story. . .

Anyway, he and Matty swapped jokes most of the evening, until the 'enforcers' arrived. . .

That's what Matty called them, the boys brought in by Brannigan from America to guard the site against the Protestant vigilantes from over the Five Crosses way. . .I was surprised to see how quickly the young lad that was with Matty made off. The leader of the 'enforcers' was Peccatini—he was an Italian American that Brannigan had brought over to organise the protection of the factory site from all the arson and things like that."

I stopped reading for a moment. "Peccatini" again. I already knew about him, because Mervyn Ritchie had mentioned him at the bar in the cricket club.

But there was something about the name that worried me. I was sure I knew nobody else of that name, and yet it somehow had a familiar ring to it. But why...?

I glanced down at the text again, and found there was more about Peccatini. So I read on, eager to find out who he was. He was rapidly becoming a central character to the whole story.

"This Peccatini was a charmer. They say that us Irish are the people with the blarney. But Peccatini could have charmed the pants off anyone, if you'll forgive the expression. He said that his grandmother had been Irish, and maybe that explained it.

Well, anyway...Peccatini, for all his smiles and charming manners, wasn't a man to beat about the bush. He spoke his mind, and he spoke it straight. Now as I have said before, I think, there were some on the Association board that said there had to be Protestants involved too, and Protestants given jobs as well. Otherwise it would just cause even worse feelings in the area than there already was. But there was strong opposition to this. One man—I don't remember who—said that up round Belfast they don't give Catholics jobs, in the shipyards and the like, so why should we give jobs to Protestants in a Catholic townland like Upperfields? I took the view myself that the most of the jobs should go to Catholics, but sure, we should have some Protestants too. Now Peccatini, he put it this way. 'Of course we have to give jobs to the Protestants...half a dozen or so.' And everyone laughed.

Now on the question of the Unionist vigilantes and their doings Peccatini was equally forthright. After they burned down the wooden huts for the workers that was to build the mill, he lost all his grace and favours, and just said: 'That'll be the last time. They have to know we mean business now.'

Anyway, when the young lad that was with Matty went out, some of the boys started whispering things in Peccatini's ear. 'Aha!' he kept repeating. 'So, it's like that, is it?'

It was only later that I learned that the lad who had left was a Protestant. I can't remember his name. And some of the boys didn't like that, that he was drinking there in a Catholic bar with Matty Coyle. And that's what they told Peccatini.

Now hard as I try I can't remember Peccatini's first name. He must have had one, and I think it was something quite ordinary for an Italian American...Something like Mario or Dario or Flavio or something like that. But for the likes of me I can't recall rightly what it was.

One more thing about Peccatini. When it came to dealing with the Unionist authorities, with the police and that, he was charm itself. Now the local police chief was a man called Burnside, a big, bluff fellow from County Antrim. And he and Peccatini seemed to get along fine, with the American always buttering him up, and Burnside always trying not to smile. And when it came to the real crisis, and the local Unionist member for Stormont, Cyril Beamish, got involved, then Peccatini and he got on like a house on fire. Which was rare, because this Beamish was a stuffed-up sort of fellow, with not much of a sense of humour. Now you'll say I took against him because he was a Protestant and a Unionist and a rich farmer. But it wasn't that. I just thought the man was very full of himself. Always expected people to bow to his command, and so forth...But he and Peccatini were thick as two thumbs, if that's the right expression. Laughing and joking together like fine ones.

'Dear me, Peccatini,' Beamish would say, 'if my old father, bless him, who was a major in the guards, if he heard us now he would turn in his grave.'

'I believe you, Mr Beamish, I believe you,' Peccatini would answer. 'And if my old man knew I was hob-nobbing with landed gentry and the police, he would want to have me shot...But then he would think better of it and reward my initiative with a new machine-gun.'

You see Peccatini liked to boast that he was a big nob when Al Capone and such people were about, and that he knew all about the criminal underworld. We were never sure we believed him, but that was the way he went on anyway. And he and Burnside and Beamish all made a big joke of it..."

"It was election time for the Stormont 'parliament', as they liked to call it, and things were getting a bit rough. The Nationalists had decided this time to make a contest of it, whatever they thought of Stormont, because they knew that if they could get everyone out to vote they had a good chance of winning. Then the question arose of who should be the Nationalist candidate, to put up against the red-faced landowner Cyril Beamish. Now secretly I would have liked to see someone like Matty Coyle put up as candidate, who was well educated and a reasonable fellow. Also he could have talked to his Protestant constituents and told them they had nothing to fear. I talked it over with one or two people, but they were too feared to support me in public, so I let the idea drop. And instead they adopted a man called Doyle from Donegal, a noisy fellow with not much brains. But he was from the Free State and I think some of them liked that because they knew it would rile the Unionists to have a Free Stater sitting in 'their' parliament...if he chose to take his seat, that is."

"It all came to a head one day when the Unionists decided to have a rally in Ballymully. Now that was a stupid enough thing to do in itself because Unionist support in the village was not that strong. Still, there were enough Protestant farmers from the country round to give them some numbers. But some of the wilder boys on our side said to themselves: this is the Unionists trying to claim that even country where they don't live has to be theirs, so we'll give them what for!

I tried myself to calm things down a bit, with a homily at mass the previous Sunday on the theme: 'Render unto Caesar that which is Caesar's'. But there weren't too many of the lads at mass that Sunday, and those that were probably didn't understand too well what I was on about and what Caesar had to do with anything, especially anything going on in Ballymully, let alone Upperfields...

So when the Unionists began their rally in a field near the Protestant church...that would be the Church of Ireland...the boys on the Catholic side started forming pickets, or so I heard, at either end of the village, to prevent people from coming and going along the main road. I don't rightly know what their line of thinking was. But it was all beginning to look a bit nasty.

I was as good as alone that day in the presbytery. Father Malone was off visiting relatives in Co. Donegal and Father McIlfatrick was too old to be of any real help.

That was why I telephoned Matty Coyle. He was one of the comparatively few people in the area at that time to have a telephone, and quite often we called each other just to have a chat. And I said to him: 'Matty, we have to do something about all this. It's getting out of hand...'"

22.

"I went out to see for myself what was happening. Now the chapel at Ballymully is on a sort of hillock in the middle of the village. The main street rises up to the front gates of the presbytery and then goes downhill again past McGonigals' the drapers and the post office and on out the road towards Derry. I found a whole crowd of people gathered outside the chapel. Some of them I knew, a lot of them I didn't know.

People were saying they expected the Unionists to try and parade right through the town, from one end to the other. And most of the people milling round outside the chapel were saying they shouldn't be allowed to, they should at least be stopped or diverted before they got to the chapel. But how they were going to be persuaded to do that was the problem. There wasn't a policeman in sight. They were obviously down with the Unionists in their field near the Protestant church. Nevertheless some obviously wanted to get in touch with the police and tell them to divert the march down the Limavady Road, so they wouldn't pass through the village and past the chapel. I volunteered to go and speak to Sergeant Murphy, if I could find him. But there were others there who argued against that. They wanted the march to come on, no doubt, so they could deal with it in their own way. And they wouldn't let me pass. Most of these, I have to say, were strangers.

After a few minutes I saw a big smart Ford car coming through the crowd, honking its horn. It pulled up near me and I could see it was empty except for the chauffeur. Then I saw who it had come for. Brannigan the factory owner was approaching up the hill, through the crowd. The men fell back on either side, obviously respectful. He was wearing a big wide-rimmed hat like he was some sort of cowboy, though I know for a fact that they don't have cowboys in Baltimore. And with him was a small figure with a dark, weasely face that I knew well.

Brannigan and the weasely man were obviously arguing.

'Peccatini,' Brannigan almost shouted at him. 'Get your men into positions where they can control this mob. I'm depending on you now. I don't want anything going wrong. It's your responsibility to keep it all under control. Otherwise who knows what will happen.'

'We're doing our best, Mr Brannigan,' said Peccatini in his nasal accent. 'But this is no army we have here. Goddammit, they don't even understand the English I speak!'

I had known Peccatini for some time, of course. He'd taken to coming to committee meetings, saying he'd been sent by Mr Brannigan. Oh a real smooth talker, he was, sure enough. 'Gentlemen,' he would say, 'Mr Brannigan has asked me to be with you today to ask, as his representative...' And so on.

Anyway, I knew him well. But that day I saw him with a different face, as it were. While Mr Brannigan was there he was as polite as can be, saying 'yes, sir' and 'no, sir' and 'three bags full, sir'. But the moment his boss was gone he spat on the ground and began muttering to himself in what must have been Italian, though it didn't sound much like the Italian I used to hear in Rome when I was there as a young priest.

Anyway, finally Peccatini went off down the hill towards the end of the village where the Unionists were having their meeting, and Mr Brannigan headed for his car. Now I wasn't at all comfortable about this 'thing' that Brannigan said might go all wrong. Was the factory owner intent on starting some mischief? Or was he doing the opposite, trying to keep control of things and stop them from taking a course of their own. I just didn't know. So I went up and appealed to him. 'Mr Brannigan,' I said. 'Can you not stay? You have won respect with these people. Can you not use your authority to help me to stop things from taking a turn for the worse. Who are all these people, anyway? Where did they come from and how are we going to disperse them?'

He gave me a real cold look. 'Father,' he said, 'if you can't keep your own people under control, how do you expect me to do it?' And then he got in his car and slammed the door and drove off. Evidently he didn't want to be seen around if there were any ructions. He was leaving it all to his man, Peccatini. And I wondered if that was wise.

I went to look for Peccatini, to ask what it was he was supposed to be 'controlling' for Brannigan. But hanged if I could find him anywhere. There were knots of men, some of them glancing at me uneasily as if they had guilty consciences, and some of them that turned their backs to me, appearing to hide some implement or other under their coats or jackets.

Slowly I became aware of a sound in the distance, a man's voice magnified by some sort of loud hailer. On and on it went, barely rising or falling, rapidly punching out word after word. It was coming from the direction of the other end of the village, near the Protestant church. . .

That, I realised, was Cyril Beamish himself, come to feed fire into the belly of his troops.

Then I noticed, in the little park near the turning off to Limavady, a man sitting astride a branch in one of the trees. He was peering in the direction of the loud-speaker voice through what looked like field-glasses. I went into the park and approached the tree. As I came closer another man, at the foot of the tree, called something up to the man with the field-glasses and at the same time quickly hid something round at the back of the tree, something long and thin, and evidently made of wood.

'Tell me,' I said to them both, 'are you Mr Peccatini's men?' I made no attempt to round the tree and find what it was the second man had been hiding. 'If so, could you let me know where he might be?'

'No, father,' said the man in the tree with a strong transatlantic accent, 'we don't know any Peccatini. No, sir, we're just simple tourists here, observing your quaint customs and folklore. . .' The man at the bottom of the tree started to smirk at that and held up his hand to his mouth to stop himself laughing.

At about that moment the machine-like voice stopped.

There was the faint sound of clapping (no cheering, I noticed, I don't think Beamish was all that popular even with the Protestants) and a moment or two later a brass band struck up, surprisingly loud. It sounded as if it was only a few hundred yards away. The Unionists must have finished their meeting. They were on the march.

I went back to the street and found, to my consternation, that it was now almost empty. The knots of men I had seen earlier had all, it seemed, disappeared. But when I walked along the street a bit I saw they had only withdrawn into the houses or alleys along either side. Meanwhile, back up the hill towards the chapel there was a whole mass of them. They were still milling round like a swarm of flies, but slowly the swarm congealed together until it formed a solid phalanx blocking the road.

Only then did I realise what was going on. They were expecting the Unionists to come up the street. And they were laying a trap for them.

I saw a man whom I recognised as one of my flock, standing with a group in an alleyway opposite and rushed over to him.

'Sean, what in the name of goodness are you doing?' I asked him. 'Why are you skulking like this in an alleyway?'

'The man said to let the Unionists through,' he said uncomfortably. 'Not to touch them.'

'So that when they come past you'll be able to trap them, no doubt!' I replied angrily. 'Just think what you're doing, man. There's going to be seriously trouble here!'

'Aye, and it's them that's causing it,' muttered one of the other men, a stranger to me, and he nodded towards the end of the village where the band was playing.

'Who's organising all this?' I demanded to know. But they all just shuffled about guiltily, or turned their backs on me.

'I think, Father,' said the stranger who had addressed me, 'you'd better go now. You don't want to get the church mixed up in all this, do you?'

I was about to give him an angry reply about the church needing to be involved in everything, but from behind me there came a shout, and then several more. 'They're coming!' I hurried back out into the middle of the street.

The Unionists' band had just turned the corner past the first houses, and the rump-a-tump of their cornets and trombones turned suddenly into a blast. It was some military marching song they were playing, loud and defiant, and demanding to be let through. Ahead of the band stomped the drum major with his staff, a big fellow dressed in some sort of blue and red military uniform, and behind him the band. And behind the band I could just make out the rows of men with their orange sashes and banners, just coming into sight around Donnelly's pub. On either side of the parade, spaced out every twenty yards or so, were black-uniformed policemen, walking along as if to guard it.

The band came on, blaring away defiantly, up the street. . .

I was lost. I just didn't know what to do.

And then something astonishing happened.

A lone figure came out of one of the side streets and started walking towards the brass band. In one hand he held a long pole—it looked like one of those things you use to open and close high windows in church halls, with a hook on the end. Anyway, on the end of this pole there was a massive great white sheet. I'll swear it was, though as a priest I know I shouldn't swear at all. It was a whole sheet. And the lonely figure with his great white banner was marching straight for the drum major. And he was waving his sheet at them and shouting, yelling at the top of his voice, over and over again. I could only make out a few of the words, during the lulls in the music.

'Go back, go back. . .or you'll get caught in a trap!. . .Stop, go home! There are hundreds waiting for you. . .! Go back!'

It was Matty. He had decided to stop them the only way he could think of.

The drum major was close to him now. No more than fifty yards between them. And I saw the big man in the blue uniform hesitate, as if he didn't quite know what to do.

Then, I think, fate (or should I say the Good Lord Himself?) took a hand. The bright and breezy march tune they were playing came to an end, and the drum major, as if by instinct, signalled with his baton for them all to halt.

The band stopped, and the procession behind them too.

'There's a trap, there's a trap!' Matty shouted through the silence. 'They're waiting for you in the alleys. Get out of here as quick as you can! For God's sake.'

A man with a flush face and whiskers, and an air of his own importance, had pushed forward through the ranks of the band. A big man, tall but also overweight, in a dark suit and tie. This was Cyril Beamish himself.

'What do you mean, man?' he shouted at Matty in a pompous voice. 'This parade expects to go right through the village, and neither you nor anyone else is going to stop it!'

I could see Matty take a deep breath. 'If you do,' he shouted, struggling now to hold the white sheet aloft in the wind, 'you will regret it, sir. There are literally hundreds of men, some of them probably armed, between here and the end of the village. And I don't think it's their intention to let you pass unmolested...'

I could see this caused quite a stir among the band members.

'We shall not be turned back...,' the important figure began, and he turned to one of the policemen nearby.

'Arrest this man,' he ordered, 'for blocking a public way...'

The policeman and two of his colleagues moved towards Matty.

But at that moment they all caught sight of something happening up the road behind him. There were now men filtering out of the side roads, little groups of them that were slowly gathering numbers, all along the street in front of the stationary band, as far as the corner where there was the little park. After that the street curved round to the left, so they couldn't see what was beyond it. But I think some of them must have guessed. Then they knew that Matty had been right.

And suddenly the important person lost all his authority. It was the drum major who did it. I don't rightly know who that fellow was, but orangeman or not, on that day he deserved a medal.

Up went his baton and a sharp order, and the whole band did an about turn. Then the drum major marched up through their ranks to what was now the front of the band. Another sharp order, the stick dropped and off they went, playing some rousing old war song.

The important figure, Cyril Beamish, was left by himself, looking foolishly at all the men in the street that he had wanted to march through. I can tell you, he didn't stay there long. He hurried back after the band, and as the musicians marched through the rest of the parade I saw all the Orangemen part to let them through, and then fall in behind them. And the policemen too. There were only about twenty of them. There was nothing they could do but walk back alongside the parade. In a minute or two they had all disappeared again, back round the corner of Donnelly's pub.

I could no longer see Matty, because of all the crowd that was now in the way. His pole with the sheet had come down without my noticing it. I hurried down the street to where he had faced up to the drum major. But when I got there I couldn't find Matty anywhere. I saw his pole, with the sheet still attached, in the drain by the side of the street. But no sign of the man himself. There were men swirling round all over the place, as if hunting for something. Who were they looking for? Obviously some of them wanted to go after the Unionists. Others seemed to be telling them that was pointless now.

And some of them were clearly wanting to find Matty.

But there was no one giving directions, no leadership. It was all chaos. Obviously whoever had organised this whole thing had not expected the Unionists to retreat. They didn't have what you might call a contingency plan. . .

Anyway, they didn't pursue the Unionists, and Beamish and his party just dispersed back into the countryside to the East of the town. And soon the crowds in Ballymully dispersed too, and there were police back on the streets. . ."

The page ended and I turned to the next one. But the narrative did not seem to flow. There was obviously a page missing. I wondered whether it had got lost by chance, or whether someone—Father O'Sullivan perhaps—might have taken it out deliberately. Irritated, I tried to pick up the story.

". . .sum total was that everybody was humiliated and angry. The Unionists had been prevented from marching through Ballymully village, as they wanted. The police chief, Burnside, was disgraced because he had failed to foresee the ambush or ensure there were adequate men in the village to protect Cyril Beamish MP and his followers. As for Beamish, well he was the most humiliated of all. He had been left standing there alone when his own followers had just upped and left him in the lurch, facing the Nationalists head on. . .

But on the Nationalist side too there were plenty of angry and humiliated men. There were many who felt cheated of their day's fun. And most of them saw Matty as a traitor, someone who had squealed to the Unionists and helped them escape what was coming to them. And the most humiliated of all, probably, though I'm only guessing this, would have been the people who organised the whole ambush idea. . .

And who were they, you may ask? Well, I don't know for certain. But I would like to bet that Peccatini fellow had a lot to do with it. And I could never rule out the suspicion that Brannigan, even though he wasn't directly responsible for it, knew well enough what his henchman was up to, and could have stopped it if he wanted. Though then, on the other hand, what I had heard outside the chapel led me to believe that Brannigan was telling Peccatini to cool things down, to drop the ambush plan. . .I was never quite sure what to believe.

Anyway, when I got the call from the hospital in Derry I went there as quickly as I could. I had to be taken to Limavady and then take the train. . .

I found him swathed in bandages, but conscious. 'Who did this to you, Matty?' I said in horror when I saw him. 'Was it our friends in black, the upholders of the law?' I asked, beginning to feel real anger. 'Or was it. . .' and I almost stopped at the shame of the thought, ' was it our own people?'

'Does it matter?' he said simply, though his swollen lips. And he just wouldn't say any more."

And that was it. There was more in Father Delaney's account, but most of it seemed to be about internal arguments on the Catholic side. And then, a few pages later, the narrative stopped. It was true then. Father Delaney had never completed his story.

I suddenly felt very tired and depressed. I put the memoirs on to the bedside table and turned off the light.

23.

On the long drive back to County Derry I had plenty of time to think about all I had discovered. On the whole it was not encouraging. I still did not know what exactly had happened on the night of Matty Coyle's death and what my father's role had been in it. What I did know was that Matty had enemies on all sides. I had now discovered that Matty had earned the hatred of the more fiery elements on the Nationalist side. Yet his actions at the Ballymully parade would have won him few friends on the Unionist side either. Particularly not with Cyril Beamish, who would see him as the man responsible for his humiliation. And as a leader of the Upperfields association he was still very much an "enemy" for the Unionists.

And I still knew very little about my father's role in all this. Yet what I did definitely know looked very ominous. My father had met Matty on the night of his death, and gone off with him into the dark. And the events that followed had left my father feeling guilty for the rest of his life.

Yet when I thought it over I decided I was now unlikely to find out any-thing more definite about the matter. And that perhaps that was all for the good. Father Delaney's memoirs had been my last hope, and the section that his friend Father O'Sullivan had given me had ended inconclusively. There had been no description of the events on the night of Matty's disappearance, no clarification of what had happened.

I had wanted to go back and question Father O'Sullivan on this, but when I rang St. Francis's they said he had gone to Dublin early that morning and they didn't know when he'd be back. I wondered if this was true, or whether the good father just didn't want to tell me any more.

In any case I was beginning to wonder how much more I really wanted to know. I was beginning to lose my nerve. There were things at play here, I realised, which had touched a raw nerve in more than one interested party. Was it wise to go digging up things in the past which could only cause more pain and ill-feeling in the present?

Enough was enough, I decided. The next day I would go and meet Ray Con-lon as arranged. He had told me he had something interesting to show me. But unless it was truly sensational, I would tell him that I was giving up the search. I would then just check out and drive back to the airport.

It was late when we came near Derry and Tim invited me to stay at his place. But I wanted to be alone, and asked him if he would drop me where I had left my car...

There was some sort of function still going on when I reached the motel near Limavady into which I had booked the previous day. As I turned into the car park there was a steady, rhythmic thumping of beat music and you could see people gyrating inside the brightly lit dining room to one side of the lobby entrance. So many cars were parked in front of the main entrance that it would have been a job to get anywhere close to the door. But I finally found a space at the furthest end of the car park, got out and locked the car.

I turned to walk to the lobby. People, as usual, had parked on the striped walkways which were meant to be kept clear for pedestrians. I had to weave my way through the vehicles, trying not to disturb their protruding wing-mirrors. I had come to the last row. There was only a narrow space to cross between the parked cars and the steps up into the lobby. I walked out into it.

I wasn't sure if it was the sudden revving of the engine that I noticed first, or the movement of the car. But I glanced sideways just in time to see the radiator grill, with unlit headlights, hurtling straight at me through the half-light.

Instinctively I jumped aside, landing with a bang on the bonnet of the nearest car. I felt a searing pain in my left arm and momentarily must have blacked out. The next thing I knew, the car's headlights flashed on as it swerved out into the road and roared off into the darkness.

There was a clatter of feet and a man's voice asked: "Are you all right? Did he hit you?"

"No," I said, wincing, "but I think my arm's broken...Could you help me inside, please?"

But even as he took hold of my good arm, I passed out.

24.

The phone rang early the next morning. I picked it up with some difficulty. I'd been told by the doctor that my arm wasn't broken, only bruised, but it hurt like hell.

It was the family lawyer from Enniskillen.

"Did you know your father was making payments of three hundred pounds a month to a bank in Derry?"

I didn't know what to say.

"Hello? Are you still there...?"

"In whose name?" I asked.

"There's no name. It was going to an account called 'McCausland family social fund'."

"He was still paying it when he died?"

"Yes."

"Can we find out who was using the account?"

"Well, it's not really within my..."

"Please. Can you try at least?"

"Well, I suppose I could make enquiries. But it will take a bit of time and effort."

"Do what you can. It's quite important."

I checked out of the motel. Too many people knew I was staying there. I tried to think who I had told about my moving there, apart from Bob and Milly. Tim McCloskey, of course, knew. And Joe Dougherty...

"Any messages?" I asked the receptionist as I paid my bill. She glanced back at my pigeon hole and pulled out not just one, but two messages. One was a white envelope with a stamp on it, the other just a slip of paper. I took them without opening or reading either.

It was the right arm I had hurt, so I could change gear and found I could just about drive, if I took things slowly. I had no clear idea of where I would go. As I exited the car park I made sure—quite sure, this time—that no one was following me, and drove up into the hills near Benbradagh. I found a lonely spot on a side-road with a lay-by for tourists, looking out across the whole broad valley of the Roe. And I sat there for an hour or more, considering what my next moves should be.

There was a stiff breeze from the North-West, and from up here you could see alternating patches of cloud and sunshine floating across the whole of County Derry and parts of Donegal. Ahead of me rose the smooth elevation of Loughermore and beyond that, to the right, the shapely mound of Slieve Snaght, out on the other side of Lough Foyle.

I found I was badly shaken by the incident the night before. It hadn't occurred to me that by stirring up the past I might be putting myself in danger. But who would want to run me down like that? The Republicans? I couldn't see quite why I was any threat to them. Unionists, maybe? Someone who had heard me talking at the cricket club? Again I could think of nothing that would have threatened anyone enough for them to want rid of me.

Perhaps, these days, people didn't need any good reason for things like that.

I needed to discuss things with someone, but whom could I trust? Young Bob, maybe? He was still annoyed with me and I wasn't sure his son, Young Robert, was the sort of person whose advice you could depend on. Should I go to the police? That would probably mean Mervyn Ritchie, and I hadn't exactly hit it off with him. Tim McCloskey? Yes, but he had told me he was busy for the next few days, catching up with things he'd missed while we were in Connaught.

So it looked as if I was stuck, for better, for worse, with Ray Conlon. I was due to meet him that morning anyway, at eleven. But I wasn't really sure about Al either. He was friendly enough. But he seemed confused himself, a passive player caught up with forces he didn't quite understand.

It was only half past nine, too early to go to my rendezvous with him. I remembered the messages I had been given at the motel. They were lying on the passenger seat beside me. I opened the first one, the slip of paper.

It was a type-written note with Ray Conlon's name at the bottom, and a scrawled signature.

"Sorry," it said, "can't make it for eleven. Can we change it to three o'clock? Same place, just by the mill run. Come on foot, if you can. Ray Conlon."

I felt a twinge of irritation. That meant another few hours to fill in. Perhaps I should just go to the airport and forget about the whole thing. I was very tempted, and even started the car, intending to set off on up over the hills to the East.

But then I switched it off again. It would be good to give Ray Conlon one last hearing. He had, after all, said he'd found an important document, a letter. Whose letter, I wondered, and sent to whom. Maybe it was a letter from Matty to Lottie which explained something about his intentions on the night he died. It also might explain just how much she knew about the affair, and whether she had played any role in it. I was annoyed that friend Al had changed the time so unexpectedly, but I supposed he must have his reasons. I wondered when he had left the message. It must have been before I arrived back from Mayo. Otherwise he could have called in to see me.

Then I remembered the second message, the white envelope.

I picked it up and examined it curiously. It had only been posted the day before, and I didn't recognise the handwriting. Still very conscious of my close encounter with the car the night before, I examined the envelope for any mysterious lumps or tiny hair-like wires. But there didn't seem to be anything suspicious about it, so I opened it carefully.

There were two sheets of paper, of different colours, one wrapped in the other. The top one was a piece of blue note-paper, with another message from Ray Conlon, this one hand-written.

"Hi there. I decided to post this copy of the 'document' to you, just in case anything happened to me on the way to our rendezvous. (Joke, of course!) Hope you get it in time. If not, I'll explain to you what it says when we meet. In either case, I think you'll find it interesting. And I do mean INTERESTING, in very big letters. There are also a few other things I have to discuss with you, things I'm not sure I understand. For example, did you know that Father Delaney definitely had a meeting with Matty Coyle, and I presume your father too, on the very night he disappeared? Anyway, more of that when we meet. In the meantime, so long and keep well. Al."

I suddenly felt really bad about my previous attitude to Ray Conlon. All along I had tended to see him as a rival, one of the 'enemy'. But in fact he was proving to be my only real friend and ally, apart from Tim.

I took up the other sheet of paper he had sent, and straightened it out. It was a single white photo-copy, the reproduction of a piece of old-fashioned note-paper, probably coloured, and ruled with faint horizontal lines. The carefully penned words hung on these lines like notes on a musical score.

Before I began reading, however, my attention was drawn to several words scrawled across the top of the page in pencil. The handwriting was markedly different from that of the letter itself. I stared at the scrawled words, suddenly filled with emotion. I recognised this handwriting.

It was my father's.

He had written, clearly after reading the letter, the words:

'Hopeless. Long live self-righteousness!'

So the letter had been written to my father!

I turned my attention to it. It was from Al Brannigan, and was obviously an answer to something my father had written:

Three Corners Inn, Upperfields 15th September, 1935.

Dear Mr McCausland,

I received your letter of 12th. Thank you for your comments.

I think we shall have to disagree about some things. The site will be opened on the 30th, and there definitely will be a priest there to add his blessing. It's all arranged now with the Bishop of Derry. . .

As for your proposal that we should hold a meeting on a neutral venue with people of influence on both sides, I'm not sure that would be very helpful. This whole thing is going ahead, and that's all there is to it. You say that a meeting might improve the atmosphere, and that we should try and stop the violence getting out of hand. But I would say to you that it's up to others, not me, to stop the violence. If you are suggesting that the people I brought in to protect property and ensure the success of the factory project have contributed to the violence, then I would deny it totally. My chief of security has given me the most categorical assurances.

You say wicked things have been done by both sides, but I'm not sure to what you are referring.

You say also that the fact you are a teacher gives you some limited influence on the unionist side, and you also mention that you are acquainted with Mr Matthew Coyle of the Development Association. Well, that's very good, Mr McCausland. And if you were able to put some of our people in touch with those who wield power on your side, it would give us a chance to say what we have to say, though I wouldn't hold out too much hope for anything coming of it. What I suggest is that you meet with Mr Coyle, and with anyone else from our side that he chooses, and you bring with you the people on your side who might be able to stop the disgraceful attacks on people's property and livelihood.

I shall inform Mr Coyle of my decision and he can get in touch with you.

Yours faithfully,

Aloysius Brannigan

At the very bottom of the page was another scribbled comment, this time not my father's and obviously written much more recently. It was in Ray Conlon's handwriting. It said:

'Was McCausland really making peace? Or were his peace overtures just a set-up? Was Matty lured into a trap?'

25.

I drove into Limavady and spent the morning at the library. Then I had lunch at a Chinese and at about half past two drove over to Banagher farm.

There didn't seem to be anyone about, so I parked my car outside the house and made for the head of the track leading down to the glen. I caught sight of Michael at a distance, coming out of one of the byres, and I waved to him.

"I won't be back for an hour or two, Michael. Tell them not to make any tea for me..."

He acknowledged my message with a wave of his hand.

Now I was pushing my way through the brambles on my way down into the glen. I wondered vaguely why Conlon had asked me to come on foot. To attract less attention, I supposed. He must have something more to tell me about my father's letter, something really interesting, since he was taking so many precautions.

The glen was strangely quiet. It wasn't just that there were virtually no insects. Summer, after all, was fast changing to autumn. There didn't seem to be any birdsong either. And though there had been a light breeze up at the farm, it didn't seem to reach into the glen. The trees stood still and silent in the heavy air, as if waiting for something to happen.

I came to the lake. Calm as a mill-pond, the expression goes, and this one certainly lived up to its reputation. Hardly a ripple on the surface. Like a mirror, reflecting the stony greyness of the sky. Through the misty air I could see the little island I had once tried to reach across the mud. From here it looked even smaller than I remembered it, a mere strip of solidified mud with a patch of reeds and several half-grown birch trees. The small strangled cries of some water bird echoed across the water, and from further up the glen came the distant squeal of a bird or animal amid the thickets. Otherwise the glen was still and lifeless.

I was now approaching the mill-house itself. Its grey outline flickered among the trunks and branches of the trees. The great iron wheel by the side of the building, repainted for the tourists, stood stiff and motionless, though from time to time I could hear it shift restlessly in its foundations and emit a hollow creaking noise. I had accepted the rendezvous at the mill because I knew nobody else would be there. Now I was beginning to regret my choice.

I crossed the stone bridge over the mill race and climbed the couple of steps to the patio with the wooden tables and benches. The tea-shop had closed for the winter the week before, but the tables were still there, presumably because there was nowhere to put them during the close season. I hoped that someone was going to cover or re-varnish them before long. Otherwise they might not survive the frequent drenchings they could expect from an Irish winter.

I looked around. No sign of Ray Conlon or anyone else. I sat for a while on one of the benches, then got up and went over to the foot of a wooden staircase I hadn't noticed before. It rose up the grey stonework of the mill house on the side facing the lake, and would no doubt give a wide view in that direction. For want of anything better to do, I began to climb the steps.

At the top was a small platform. I paused there for a moment and looked back out across the lake. It had become so misty that it was now difficult to see the dim forms of the trees and bushes at the far end.

I turned to the door that led off the platform and tried the handle. To my surprise it was open. I pushed on the door and went in.

The room beyond was completely bare, except for a few empty tea chests and some ragged posters on the walls advertising festivals or concerts. It seemed the room had been used, and not so long ago, as part of the tea-house. The floor was of polished wood and the walls had been decorated, I guessed, no more than a year or two previously. But obviously business had not been sufficient to keep the room open this last summer.

I went back out to the wooden balcony. Once again I was struck by the peace and quiet of the place. Almost as if someone had decreed a reverend hush. The only sound other than the wild birds was the gentle gurgle of the water as it disappeared under the little stone bridge into the mill race. I looked down at the water, to where the lake narrowed, and my eyes followed the flow of the water towards the narrow channel that led to the bridge.

Just where the channel swept under the bridge it was barred by a metal grill. Clogged in the grill was an untidy collection of broken branches, reeds and other flotsam which had floated in from the lake. And among all the rubbish was what I took to be a large log which bobbed up and down in the water with a strange, jerky motion.

It took me several moments to realise that the branch protruding from this log was in fact a human arm, and the white patch on its end a hand.

At the very second I recognised the body for what it was I heard the crunch of tyres on the gravel car park round the corner. I'd just reached the bottom of the wooden stairs when two dark figures came round the corner of the house.

"There's...there's somebody caught in the mill run," I stuttered, waving desperately towards the bridge. "It looks...It looks as if he's dead."

"It's a he, is it?" said a third figure as it came round the corner. "Perhaps you'd better show us where he is."

It was Mervyn Ritchie, the local DS.

I was annoyed by his tone. "Look," I said, "I've only just spotted the body, from up there on the platform. I don't know it's a he. I'm just guessing..."

"Well let's go and see if you're right," said Ritchie with irritating composure. It was as if he had expected to come and find somebody dead at the mill.

I hurried over to the bridge, and looked down, suddenly full of fear. I was joined a moment later by the two uniformed policemen, and by Ritchie.

From this angle we could see the face behind the arm, and whose it was.

"You were meeting him here, were you?" asked Ritchie grimly. I could see Ray Conlon's features quite clearly. His eyes were still open. They were staring lifelessly back towards the lake, with a look of surprise and fear.

I pulled away from the parapet, and stood staring helplessly at the misty outlines of the trees beyond the water. Why did Ray have to be looking back towards the lake? Was that where he had been killed, before he was swept into the mill race by the current?

They probably killed him, a malign voice said within me, at the same spot where they killed Matty.

I shook myself, literally, to get rid of such thoughts. The men who had killed Matty were all long dead. Whoever had murdered Ray was very much alive and, I suddenly realised, a very real danger to me.

I turned back to Ritchie, who was still staring down at Ray's body.

"Yes, I was supposed to meet him here at eleven this morning. But then I got a message, asking me to come at three o'clock instead..."

"Oh yes. And who was this message from?"

I frowned at him.

"Well, I assumed it was from Conlon himself...The receptionist just gave me...a printed message."

"And did you ask who had left it at the motel?"

"Well, no...I..."

"You assumed...Assumptions, assumptions! It wouldn't be the first time that assumptions were the death of someone."

"So...you do believe me? You believe that I only arrived here a few minutes ago?"

"How many minutes exactly?"

"Well, ten...fifteen? It's difficult to say."

He looked at me with his dry, sceptical eyes. "Difficult to say, is it?" He walked to the other side of the bridge and stared down again at poor Ray's body, bobbing helplessly in the stream.

"Well, if you have to know," he said, "the answer is yes."

"Yes what?"

"Yes, I do believe your story. Though another might well not...When was the last time somebody saw you?"

I stared at him for a moment, before I understood the question. "Well, maybe half an hour ago, Michael Fallon was up at the farm when I parked there..."

"Fallon, eh? Is he the only one who can vouch for you...?"

"But why are you here?" I asked. "How did you know something was wrong?"

"A message, delivered at the station by a small boy. Printed, just like yours."

After a pause he added: "Let's hope, for your sake, that the messages were printed on the same machine...It might help you in a courtroom."

26.

I didn't stay the night at the farm, though Milly urged me to. When one of Ritchie's men finally dropped me there, after a cursory interrogation in the back of a police car, I thanked Milly for her kindness and drove off to find a bed and breakfast. I felt vulnerable at the farm, and far too close to the twice-cursed glen. I also wanted to be alone for a while. But I rang the farm in the morning. It was Young Robert who answered.

"What's going on, Adrian? Was that Conlon fellow not the one you said you met last week?"

"Yes, Robert. But I'm all right, I assure you…Has anyone been looking for me?"

"Mervyn Ritchie rang. He wants to know where you are…You have to go in and give evidence again."

"Yes, all right, I'll phone him…Anyone else?"

"There's a woman been asking for you," he said. "She rang twice. Says it's urgent."

"A woman?" I said, mystified. "Did she leave a name?"

"No, but she left a number. I've got it here…wait a moment."

I rang the number, thinking it might be one of the librarians at Limavady. But the voice that answered was certainly no librarian's. It sounded weary, on guard, hostile.

"This is Adrian McCausland. Did someone try to ring me from that number?"

There was a moment's silence. Then she said: "Yes, it was me."

"I'm sorry," I said, "but do I know you?"

"It's Shenagh Kelly…You know, that looks after Lottie Coyle."

"Yes, Shenagh, I remember only too well…What can I do for you?"

"She wants to see you."

I hesitated. "Are you sure? The last time I was there she didn't seem to want me there at all. And you more or less kicked me out for giving her bad memories…"

"I know, I know. I'm sorry. But she says she wants to see you now. Urgently. She apologises about the last time. But she couldn't speak openly. She was afraid. Afraid of them."

"Who exactly are they? You mean Sean Hill and his associates?"

"It's better not to mention names over the phone."

I remembered making my rendezvous with Ray Conlon by phone, and knew she was right.

There was a pause.

"You know that someone has been killed," I said. "Ray Conlon, the American who came to see Lottie before me?"

Her strained voice now became even hoarser. "Yes, I know. That's one of the reasons Lottie wants to see you. She says you could be in danger too."

"From whom? From Joe Dougherty? Or his friend Sean Hill?"

"I'm not saying anybody's name," she insisted. "Not over the phone. Phones can be listened to, you know."

"Okay," I said, "so how can I meet her?"

"You'll have to come here again."

"Tim McCloskey's out of town..."

"Can't you drive yourself? It's not hard to find. Buncrana Street."

I didn't like the idea of driving alone into the Bogside, and said so.

"What are you worried about?" she said caustically. "Do you think we eat people here or something? We're not cannibals, you know..."

But she agreed to ask her son to meet me and take me there.

***

I had been at the appointed spot on the Diamond for at least ten minutes, looking nervously at the people walking up from Shipquay Street, when I felt someone tap my shoulder.

"Mr McCausland is it?" I turned to find myself confronted by two youths, both of them poorly shaven and in woolly hats. One of them took the cigarette out of his mouth and, seeing my confusion, said: "Oh don't worry! I'm Brendan Kelly, all right, come to collect you. And this is only Liam, my mate. He's come along to give you added reassurance!"

And the two exchanged a smirk.

"Car's down this way, if you want to come," said Brendan. "Couldn't park it thataway," he nodded towards the Protestant cathedral, "cos that's the Fountain and it's full of Prods. We wouldn't be safe there." He and Liam both chortled. I followed them down along the street and under Bishop's Gate. His car was a surprisingly flashy Japanese number, with only two doors. I was invited to get into the back seat.

"Good protection, you see," said Liam, leering at me. "No one can pull you out without us knowing!" I was beginning to tire of his little jokes.

Brendan turned the key and we sped off down through the narrow streets into the Bogside. It took us less than five minutes to reach the familiar door of Shenagh's house.

"Do you think it's safe to let him out now, Liam?" asked Brendan.

"Aw I don't know, Brendan. There's a few dodgy looking characters wandering around."

The street was, in fact, empty.

"Okay, lads," I said as amiably as I could. "You've had your joke. I won't get lost from here on in."

"So long, then," said Brendan cheerily as he got back into the car. "Hope you can find your way home!" And I heard their cackles of laughter as the car sped off. Shenagh had already opened the door to let me in.

27.

Lottie was sitting in the same straight-backed chair by the window. But as soon as I entered the room I could see there was something different about her.

"Leave us, Shenagh," she said softly, but in a voice that was totally under control. Shenagh frowned, but did as she was told.

Lottie was a different person. Maybe the last time she had been on some sort of sedative, or maybe, as I had strongly suspected, her 'dottiness' had been at least partly an act. Now she was altogether more composed.

"Sit down," she said gently. "Sit down here beside me, so I can see you."

She was looking at me in a strange, wistful way. "So you're Lexie's boy," she said, a sad smile touching her features.

"Yes, we met before, when I came..."

"Yes, yes, I know. But I couldn't speak then. I couldn't say anything. There was that man McCloskey with you..."

"Tim? But Tim was surely someone you could trust?"

"Don't trust any of them. Specially if they want your vote..." She gave a little cackle, but then sighed. "You never know these days who you can trust and who you can't...You see, I've always been told, all my life, that I mustn't speak unless I'm told to...And I have, fool that I am, always done what they've told me. But now I've had enough. And you're Lexie's son, so I'm going to tell you things they don't want known. The same things I told that other fellow, the American. But you've got to be careful! You've got to be very, very careful..."

I leaned forward. "Lottie, I've already seen Al Brannigan's letter to my father, after he suggested a meeting. Conlon sent me a copy, before he died. But can I ask...how you came to have that letter?"

She seemed to become flustered and confused. She looked away, and started fidgeting with the tissue she was holding.

"We were friends, your father and me..." She thought for a moment, and then said: "We were very close."

"You were...his girl friend?" I asked, astonished.

She didn't seem to hear the question. When she looked back at me she seemed to have forgotten what we were talking about.

"Lexie was the only one Matty trusted, you see. He was the only one of the Prods that poor Matty would ever have trusted."

Tears were now beginning to appear in her pale, tired eyes. "Matty trusted your father," she repeated.

Why did she keep saying that? I asked myself.

"Lottie," I said, "from Brannigan's letter we know that my father suggested a meeting with him, and that Brannigan decided to send Matty. But can you tell me anything more about that meeting? You told me the last time that my father went off alone with Matty..."

"Yes," she murmured, "Matty went off to McCauslands' house, to collect your father and go on to their meeting..."

"And they went off to the Glen, did they, to the mill house? But was anybody else supposed to be there, at the meeting?"

"Yes, there were supposed to be other people, but I don't rightly know who they were. I know they talked about asking the priest...what was his name? I always forget his name..."

"Father Delaney? So he was at the meeting too, was he?"

"I don't know...I think he was supposed to be there. But I don't know if he went in the end. Matty said Father Delaney wasn't sure about coming..."

I was beginning to feel frustrated. I was so near and yet so far.

"So who else, Lottie, was supposed to be there, at the meeting? Did Matty ever say anything about that? Who was supposed to be there from the Protestant side, for example?"

She shook her head. "All I know is they wanted to invite one or two other people to this meeting, from either side. And Matty and your father quarrelled over it. When Matty got to the McCauslands' house there was a big row...Everyone in the farm must have heard it. Your father told me this later. I think it was when your father told Matty who he had invited."

"Matty didn't like who it was..."

"No..."

"So who was it?" I pressed her.

She just went on shaking her head. "Your father would never tell me. Said it was better I didn't know."

"But it must have been people who had some influence, people who could try and stop the violence from getting worse..."

Lottie sighed. Her voice was getting weak and tired.

"You would think so, wouldn't you..."

"Lottie, please try to think...If we know their identity it will bring us much closer to knowing who it was killed Matty!"

She turned her sunken eyes towards me and for the first time there was scorn and annoyance in her look.

"You don't think...You don't think I haven't thought about it for every hour...of every day I've lived ever since?" she said in a voice cracking with emotion. "But your father told me once: never go throwing accusations around. That's why he never told me nothing. So I wouldn't make accusations and get myself into trouble…which is what I always used to do. When I was young…"

I said nothing for a while, to allow her to calm down. Then I asked, gently:

"Did Al Brannigan go to the meeting after all, do you think?"

"I don't know," she said. "You saw for yourself, he told your father in the letter that he wouldn't go…But you never know, maybe he changed his mind for some reason…"

"Or maybe Brannigan sent somebody else to represent him. Maybe the man he brought over from America as his 'security chief'. What was his name…Peccatini?"

"I heard that name. But neither your father nor Matty spoke well of him. They wouldn't have wanted him there."

She seemed very sure on that point.

"And from the Protestant side," I prompted her, "who would they have asked? The police chief maybe? Burnside I think his name was. He would certainly have had an interest in keeping the peace. Or someone connected with Beamish, the MP? Did Beamish have an assistant or a secretary he might have sent, do you know?"

Again she shook her head. Clearly she had no idea who had been at the meeting.

"All I know," she said finally, "was that one of them wasn't supposed to be there?"

That confused me. "What do you mean, Lottie? Do you mean that he wasn't invited…"

She nodded vigorously. "He wasn't welcome, this one, and afterwards, when it was all over and done with, your father was always very agitated about the fact he came."

"But my father never said who it was?"

"No…No, he didn't."

I got up and started to walk round the room, to help me to think.

"So somebody came to the meeting who wasn't invited. Yet someone must have told him, or her, about the meeting…"

"Yes, there was a traitor. Your father always said there was a traitor at the meeting…"

"One traitor, and the person he invited. So two people were trying to disrupt the others' efforts to bring peace. But who were they, Lottie? Who were they? It's very important we find out…"

She just looked blank. After a few moments she said to me:

"I think you'd better go now. I'm feeling tired."

"Is there nothing more you can tell me, Lottie? About what happened that night?"

"Nothing I think I want to tell you," she said in little more than a whisper, looking town at her twisted, arthritic hands.

I waited a moment longer, standing beside her, disappointed that she hadn't been able to tell me more, not wanting to believe there wasn't something else she might have forgotten. But she seemed now to be nodding off, tired out perhaps by her efforts to coax up memories from the distant past. I laid my hand gently on her shoulder, and left.

On the way out Shenagh took me aside into her kitchen.

"I don't know if she told you this," she said, "but Lottie had a child…when she was a young thing. That's why they sent her to Mayo, not because she was weak in the head."

I nodded. "Yes, I'd guessed that. And when I went down to Mayo recently I did some checking. It was a boy. But Father O'Sullivan told me, when I rang him to ask, that it died at the age of three."

Shenagh looked at me doubtfully, as if wondering whether to say any more.

"It didn't die," she said finally. "It's still alive. Very much so."

I looked at her in astonishment. "So…who?"

"No, no," she said hurriedly. "I've said enough. I've promised Lottie never to tell. But I just wanted to warn you."

28.

Tim drove like a madman. His battered Citroen squealed round the corners of the narrow, undulating road, leaving very little room for anything else coming the other way.

"Sure no one uses this road much," he said cheerfully as he saw my grip on the door handle tighten for the umpteenth time. "Just a few farmers and people who live up the valley beyond the reservoir..."

A moment or two later he added: "Poor old Ray Conlon won't be using it any more, that's for sure."

We came to a point in the dipping, winding road where the hazel thickets thinned and we got a view of the ugly concrete mass of the dam, straight in front of us. Tim pulled into a small parking area beside the road.

"Built in the 30s," Tim noted formally. "Provides Derry with most of its drinking water."

I surveyed the grim walls of the dam. Grey, unyielding, and yet not totally invulnerable. There had been at least one attempt to blow up a reservoir, early in the troubles, and now there was barbed wire all round it. And floodlights at night.

Then we were back in the car and climbing steeply through the trees, twisting round the side of the valley until we were level with the top of the great concrete barrier. Behind it the grey surface of the reservoir lake was broken by a steady breeze from the West. We were past the dam now, on an open slope, among small, rush-ridden fields marked off by untidy stone walls. To the left the ground rose steadily to the heather and bracken of a low mountain ridge. And to the right lay the silver strip of the reservoir, its long finger pointing crookedly up through the brown foothills to the higher peaks to the south.

"Conlon's place is a mile or two up the road," Tim informed me. "We need to look for an iron gate leading off up the hill to the left. In some trees, just beyond a bridge."

We dropped into a wooded hollow and negotiated a narrow stone bridge. Then the road turned sharply and began to rise again. The metal gate suddenly loomed into sight on the left. It was painted green, and blocked off an untarred but well-kept lane that rose steeply through the trees. I jumped out and opened the gate for Tim to drive through.

"Leave it open till I come back," he said, and I nodded, getting back in the car. We drove on up the lane and out of the trees. The lane continued to rise between rough stone walls, though not so steeply now, heading towards a house that was just visible behind a copse of fir trees. As we approached I saw to my surprise that it was a modern bungalow, set in its own small rock garden. A haven of tranquillity and human endeavour in this otherwise bleak and hostile setting.

There were steps leading up through the garden to the front door. Tim stopped the car in the gravel space at their foot and handed me a bunch of keys.

"There's a Chubb and a Yale which double-locks," he said. "DS Ritchie and his men finished with the place a couple of days ago, it seems. They told the landlord he was free to re-let it any time he wanted."

"And you're sure Conlon's books and research materials are still there?" I asked anxiously.

"So Mr Heaney said. Told me the police weren't much interested in them... He's trying to contact the family in America to ask what he should do with the things Ray left here."

"What family did he have? Was he married?"

"No. No wife, no children. Just brothers and sisters, it seems."

Well, maybe that was a minor blessing, I thought.

Tim turned the car and gave me a cheery wave as he set off back down the lane. He had decided not to join me in my search. He told me frankly he thought I was on a wild goose chase. He would use the time, he said, to look up a couple of his party contacts in the vicinity. The ancient red Citroen sped back down the narrow lane and disappeared over the crest into the tree-filled hollow beyond. I heard the engine slow down to pass through the gate, and accelerate again as Tim turned on to the road. Then I started to climb the steps towards the bungalow.

I locked the front door behind me and began to explore. It wasn't difficult to locate the room Ray Conlon had used as his study. It was to the left of the small entrance hall, with a bay window looking out over the valley. The desk stood in the bay itself, facing the window, with a clear view of the narrow strip of water directly beneath and the dark hills climbing up on the other side.

On the desk and the floor around it were untidy piles of books and files, and here and there miscellaneous papers arranged in no apparent order. I examined them closely, but there seemed to be no logic in the way they had been placed. Perhaps the police had re-arranged them.

In the middle of the large oak desk itself lay a note-pad, and a still open fountain pen. The note-paper was familiar. It was the blue paper he had used to write his last note to me, enclosing the copy of Aloysius Brannigan's letter. I wondered if the original of that letter was still here, hidden among the haphazard documents around me. Or had someone else already claimed it? The same someone who was, I was now convinced, trying to prevent the full truth about the Brannigan's mill affair from ever becoming public.

I looked round the room again, and my eye came to rest on a dark object in one corner. I went over towards it and saw that it was the case for a lap-top computer, lying open on the floor. If there was a case, I reckoned, there must also be a computer.

Yet there was no immediate sign of one. I searched high and low for it, in cupboards and drawers, and under piles of folders. Then I went into the next room, to see if it were there.

I finally found it in the bedroom at the back of the house, beside the bed. Obviously he had been working on it until late in the night.

I brought it back into the study, put in on the desk and plugged it in. If I was going to find anything, I decided, it would be here. When the icons appeared I clicked on 'my documents'. There were only eight of them, but they all had the title 'Upperfields' and a number.

I was in luck! The fruits of Ray Conlon's research had not been lost.

***

Soon I was deep in the first file. Ray Conlon certainly did not beat about the bush. There was a short historical introduction, and then, as the opening to his first chapter, he had written:

"The shirt factory at Upperfields would have given direct employment to at least 200 people. That means it would have sustained up to a thousand people, if you include families and support industries. It would have made that quarter of County Derry a beacon of prosperity amid the grey landscape of the depression…"

Over-stated and a bit far-fetched, I thought, but probably not that far from the truth.

"The collapse of the project meant the destruction of many hopes and the ruination of many lives. Those responsible bear a heavy burden of responsibility for the continuing poverty of the region, and the continuing emigration…"

Hey, hey, Ray, steady on a bit, I thought. This is a bit over the top, isn't it? I went out of that file, which seemed to be mostly background and rather broad generalisations, and went into the second. This, I found, was very much more to the point.

"…The single most important factor in the collapse of the shirt factory project was the murder, yes, I dare call it the murder, of the popular figure and leader of the Defence Association, Matty Coyle. So it would be fair to say that if we can identify those responsible for his death, we can also find those who destroyed the project of the Upperfields mill…"

125

Would it? I thought to myself. Would it be fair to say that? This, I concluded, might have been Ray Conlon's initial impression. But even he seemed to have developed doubts after he had written it. He had added in brackets a little note:

"Re-write this bit. It's a bit too bald. Bring in the factors I've since discovered. . ."

So it seemed Ray was ready, as any true researcher should be, to constantly revise his ideas as his search for the truth advanced. All due credit to him, I thought. . .

I worked at the desk for the rest of the morning, and all afternoon, glancing up only occasionally to observe how the weather was changing. The bright and breezy morning with its clear blue interludes and ragged, driven clouds was yielding to a uniform greyness, and then an ever darkening sky to the West.

At one stage I heard the whine of a motor, and subconsciously assumed it was an electric saw somewhere down the valley below the dam. But then it became clear, as the high-pitched sound drew closer, that it was in fact a motor-bike, evidently being driven at some speed.

29.

I paused from my reading to listen. But the sound, which had risen and fallen in intensity as it progressed up the twisting, rolling road, then became duller and finally stopped quite abruptly while it was still, I reckoned, some way off. The silence that followed made me suddenly aware of the wind. It had risen significantly, and the sashes on the bay windows in front of me were starting to rattle gently. When I looked out over the lake I saw that the breeze was beginning to bend the upper limbs of the trees that lined the shore, while out over the lake the hills in that direction had disappeared in a blank greyness which indicated the imminent approach of rain.

I switched on the desk lamp and rose to pull across the curtains, trying to shut out the gathering gloom.

I had plugged the laptop into the small printer already installed on the desk, and had printed off each of Ray Conlon's files as soon as I had skimmed through it. I wanted an accurate record of his findings, hard copy that I could browse through at leisure later on. Now as the whirring of the printer stopped after the fourth file was on paper, I thought I heard the sound of the motor-bike engine suddenly sparking back into life, and the muffled whine as it retreated down the valley.

Strange, I thought. I wonder where the rider has been all this time. I hadn't noticed any houses, or indeed side-roads, between the dam and the turn-off for Conlon's house. But I didn't give it much thought. I was wrapped up in the notes on the computer and what they were telling me.

I kept thinking of what Lottie had told me the day before. Matty and my father had quarrelled over who had been invited to the meeting to discuss peace moves. My first conclusion was that it must have been a Protestant, because it was Matty who had objected. Then there had been a traitor at the meeting, and he had told someone else of its location and venue, someone who had come to the meeting, but who was not welcome—to either Matty or my father. This time my chief suspects were Brannigan himself, and Peccatini his henchman…But I had absolutely no proof. Would Ray's notes reveal anything about who had actually attended the meeting?

In the fifth file I came across a series of notes concerning the 'security men' brought in to Upperfields by Brannigan.

"Peccatini's men were described as 'hoodlums' and 'gangsters' by Cyril Beamish and the Unionist press, but there is no evidence to prove this (keep checking).

Their involvement in the whole affair, as far as I can ascertain, was confined to the following:

1) *They stopped and turned back (politely and firmly, Peccatini said) a truck carrying a dozen Loyalist youths on the road from Dernafleck to Upperfields (26th August).*

2) *Two of them were involved in a brawl at a bar in Limavady (Protestant district?). Remanded on bail.*

3) *They played an unknown part in the events at Ballymully when Nationalists tried to prevent a Unionist march through the village.*

4) *One of them (Father O'Sullivan said his name was Reilly) was caught by a Catholic farmer (Donaghy) canoodling with his daughter. Reilly was sent home to America.*

5) *A totally unexplained affair somewhere in the Bovevagh area, which resulted in the deaths of two Protestant farm labourers. The 'Peccatini mob', as they were dubbed by the Unionists, were somehow held responsible, but there is no clear evidence either of what happened there or of any involvement by Peccatini's men. My own feeling is that this was pure propaganda by the Unionists...*

6) *The Matty Coyle affair...(???)"*

Once again, the three question marks had obviously been added later, evidence that Ray Conlon might have been revising his opinion on what its true significance was. Clearly he believed that Peccatini and his men had played some role in the Matty Coyle affair. But what was that role? Ray had left no indication.

Outside, the rain had now begun in earnest. As it began drumming heavily on the bungalow roof I was suddenly conscious of how late it was. Tim had told me he would be back at about six o'clock. It was now almost seven thirty.

What was keeping him? I was stuck here until he got back. I got up and made myself a cup of tea from the things left in the kitchen. Then I read on.

The early files had been written up into complete chapters. The later ones, in contrast, were noticeably short on detail.

"Ironically," I read in the seventh file, *"beginning of construction at the Upperfields site began on the very same day the election campaign started. Unionists immediately made a big fuss. A priest (Father Delaney underlines that it was not him—why not, I wonder?) invited to bless the construction site. This, said Unionists, was proof that it was all a big Catholic plot and the intention was to employ only Catholics...As election day approached and work on the site proceeded, tension obviously increased. From Father Delaney's account, and elsewhere, I've been able to trace twelve 'incidents' in the immediate vicinity of Upperfields: sheds burning down, stealing of vehicles and farm animals, etc.. Seven of them were attributable to Protestant gangs, five possibly to Catholics..."*

The eighth and final file I found the most frustrating. It was full of cryptic notes, difficult to interpret, like:

"Peccatini and Burnside—big public row outside Dungiven courthouse. But others got on well. I wonder why?"

And then, a bit later:

"Father D lays it on a bit thick. But his suspicions can't totally be dismissed."

And the most infuriating reference of all:

"Father D's account of the meeting. That holds the clue, I'm sure. . ."

I did not hear the car approaching. The first I was aware of it was when the flowered curtains in front of me caught the reflection of its headlights. A few moments later I heard the gentle scrunch of its tyres on the gravel driveway below the house. I went on working, expecting Tim to come up and ring the doorbell. Instead, there was an impatient parp from the car's horn.

I got up and pushed back the curtain. I had forgotten that it was pouring. All I could see was the thick, dancing curtain of water slanting across the rock garden, and the two white beams carved by the headlights through the driving rain.

I waved my hand vaguely at the car and went to unplug the lap-top. Stuffing my print-outs hurriedly into an inside pocket of my coat, and the laptop into its case, I took a last glance round the room. Then I switched off the desk-lamp. The room was now illuminated solely by the eerie reflection of the vehicle's lights, projecting strange jerky shadows of the rain drops on to the opposite wall.

I let myself out of the front door and for several moments stood struggling to lock it behind me. Then, picking my way cautiously down over the slippery concrete of the steps, I made my way towards the car.

The driver opened the door for me, and thankfully I collapsed into the front passenger seat.

"Nice weather we're having, isn't it?" said Tim's cheerful voice. "Find what you were looking for?"

"Mm," I said. "I found something very interesting, anyway. Whether it's what I was looking for exactly I'm not sure."

"Just so long as it keeps you happy," Tim replied, and turned the car round in the cramped parking space. A moment or two later we were speeding down the lane, far too fast for my comfort. Tim saw my unease again.

"Don't worry, man," he said. "I once took part in the Round Ireland Rally!"

"Mm, well we're not in a race just at the moment, Tim."

He swept down the slope into the trees and we came to the painted gate, still lying open, the way I had left it that morning. Tim drove through and stopped on the road.

"Was it you who opened the gate this afternoon?" Tim asked casually as he undid his seat-belt.

"No," I said in surprise. "We left it open this morning, remember?"

"Ah, but I closed it again when I left. And it was lying open when I came back...Anyway, gate's on my side this time. My turn to get wet!"

And he jumped out briskly before I could say anything.

Alarm bells suddenly began ringing in my head. "Tim!" I called, and I began to take off my seat-belt. "We don't have to close it."

But he was already back at the gate and pulling it shut. It groaned ever so slightly on its hinges as it swung back behind him.

I distinctly heard the click as the metal rod slid back into place. But I had no recollection of any sound after that. There was a blinding flash, and the dark shape of Tim's body hit the rear window on the driver's side.

I was thrown sideways and hit my head on the window. Everything went dark.

30.

"You've an unfortunate habit of always turning up at the scene of the crime," DS Ritchie said drily.

He was watching me sip gingerly from the hot cup of tea a medic had handed me. The rain had eased, but was still falling diagonally across the lights of the parked vehicles. "Everywhere you go there's carnage. Anyone would think you were part of the plot."

"I think I *am* part of the plot…but not in the way you imply."

"Oh, I wasn't implying anything," he replied in his annoyingly high-pitched voice. "I think you're very much part of the plot. But I'm trying to figure out just how and why."

"I don't suppose that Tim…?"

He shook his head. "Hadn't a chance. And you don't want to see the state he's in…So tell me again, because you weren't very coherent before. Just why exactly were you up here at Conlon's place? Everything in that house is still evidence, you know?"

"Tim told me you'd finished searching it. And you'd given the keys back to the landlord."

"That doesn't give you the right to go blundering round up there. I've a good mind to charge you with tampering with evidence…if we can't find anything else to charge you with!"

A paramedic appeared out of the double beam of the ambulance headlights. "Look, this man is in no fit state to be questioned," he told Ritchie. "Can't you wait till we get him back for a check-up."

"This man," snapped Ritchie, "keeps appearing where there are dead bodies. And I would like to know why!" He threw the styrofoam cup he had been clutching into the hedge and stalked off.

"Thanks," I said to the medic.

"No problem," he said. "I've come across Ritchie before…He pulled in my brother-in-law for questioning just because he went to Gaelic football matches. At least, that's all they could prove…"

"I suppose he has to try and do his job," I muttered. I still wasn't thinking very clearly.

The medic looked at me ironically.

"If you say so," he said shortly, and then he too walked off into the darkness.

The time has come, I thought as we jolted along in the ambulance back towards civilisation, to bring this whole thing to a close. Things, as my father would have said, have gone 'way beyond the linen green'...

But I didn't intend to just run away. I wanted to bring it to a head. Let them do their worst, whoever they were.

But to bring it to a head I would somehow have to persuade all the parties involved to come together. As Matty had, on that last fateful night. Arrange a meeting between the main protagonists. And maybe count on one or two uninvited guests coming along as well...

I made a sudden decision. It was the only answer. A meeting to confront the issues, to bring the conflicting parties face to face, to force all the festering pus of decades into the open air.

So whom would I invite? I realised I already had the list ready in my head.

And where would this fateful rendezvous take place?

There was only one place I could think of.

31.

"How did you know I was hereabouts?" Father O'Sullivan asked me, turning round from the front seat of the car. With his rimless glasses and pursed lips he looked even more like Eamon de Valera than when I had first met him.

"I phoned St. Francis's. They told me you'd gone to County Derry, and then I made further enquiries with the Ballymully presbytery."

"Well you were lucky to catch me. Father Donnelly and I have to get back to Mayo this evening." He nodded towards the heavily built young priest who was driving the battered old 60s beetle.

"I'm very grateful to you for agreeing to meet," I said.

We were on the hill descending into Upperfields. I had driven to Young Bob's farm and asked Father O'Sullivan to pick me up from there so we could continue together to our destination. Strange, I thought even as I was making the arrangement, how I'm seeking protection from a Catholic priest.

"Could I ask just what the purpose of this meeting is, Mr McCausland?" Father O'Sullivan asked. "You were quite secretive on the phone. It's a strange sort of venue, and as I say, we still have a long journey to make back to Mayo."

"It shouldn't take too long," I assured him. "Maybe an hour or so. It all depends on whether the other guests arrive on time."

We crossed the hump-backed bridge and turned into the car park beside the Three Corners Inn.

"You'll accept the offer of a pint now, won't you?" said Father Donnelly. "You look as if you could do with one."

I really was not very keen. This particular pub made me nervous.

"We can begin to discuss matters here," Father O'Sullivan supported his colleague, "and then go on to the other place, if you insist. As they say, a wee bit of alcohol helps the flow of conversation..."

Reluctantly I agreed. "Just one pint then," I said.

I suppose I had expected the interior of the pub to be full of republican slogans and tricolours, with sinister, ill-shaven men hunched over their beers whispering conspiratorially. In fact we entered a perfectly normal saloon bar, with only a few customers dotted around the spacious room. The only thing which indicated it might not be just any bar was what appeared to be a small shrine in one corner, with a celtic cross and several photographs, presumably of the dead hunger-strikers.

We settled by a window looking out on to the car park.

"So, can you give us any idea what this is all about, Mr McCausland?" Father O'Sullivan asked again. "You said you wanted me to meet some other people, in a particular venue. I have to say, I thought twice before coming..."

"Yes, I understand that," I said, taking a long gulp of my pint. Perhaps it had been a good idea to come into the inn, after all. I had arranged to meet Father O'Sullivan earlier than the others. Apart from the protection I felt he gave, I wanted to make sure whose side he was on.

"And since you're about the only one of my 'guests' that I trust in any way, I think I can tell you something about it before we go and meet the others..."

I paused. A group of young men had entered the bar, laughing and joking loudly. They glanced curiously at the three of us, but when they saw the two priests they carried on to the bar. One of them even nodded his head in greeting.

"You don't mind Father Donnelly being in on this?" Father O'Sullivan asked. "I've told him one or two things..."

"No, no, the more the merrier," I said, glancing at Father Donnelly's sturdy frame. It might well be a good thing to have him around, I thought.

"It's like this, you see," I began. "I've asked four people to meet together this afternoon. All four, I'm convinced, know a lot more about Matty Coyle and what happened to him than they're willing to admit...at least to me."

The grey-haired priest was watching me intently with his probing eyes. "Go on," he said.

"You, for example, Father O'Sullivan...You told me that Father Delaney's record of events had never been finished. The text you gave me broke off just when it was getting interesting. And yet..." I took a deep breath. "I believe that he did complete it, and that you showed the finished version to Ray Conlon."

Father Donnelly glanced over at his elder colleague to gauge his response.

"What on earth brought you to that conclusion?" asked Father O'Sullivan. His face showed surprise and amusement, but also a touch of annoyance. And his eyes narrowed behind the rimless glasses. "Did Ray Conlon tell you that?"

"No...he never got the chance. But among his own notes about the Upperfields affair are references to things he said were in Father Delaney's memoirs, but which I couldn't find in the parts you gave me."

"For example?" he said coolly.

"For example, details of incidents which took place in and around Upperfields at that time. Attacks on people and property carried out by both sides..."

Father O'Sullivan made a dismissive noise. "He could have found those anywhere..."

"But he specifically attributed them to Father Delaney," I interrupted him. After a moment or two he asked: "What else?"

"Ray Conlon had read Father Delaney's account of the final meeting, here at the mill house, between himself, my father and Matty...and at least two others. Yet none of this was in the material you gave me."

I was fishing here. Ray had indicated that such an account existed. But it hadn't been clear from his notes whether he had actually read it. I was hoping Father O'Sullivan wouldn't guess that.

His face clouded and lost some of its good humour. "How did you get access to Dr Conlon's notes?" he asked, just a little shortly.

"With the help of my late friend Tim McCloskey," I said pointedly.

"Ah yes, a sad business..." He looked down at the table.

I knew that the crucial moment had come. Would Father O'Sullivan concede, or call my bluff? He looked up at me, folded his arms in a very deliberate way and leaned backwards, as if preparing to take a defiant stand. His face had hardened. I was convinced, at that moment, that I had lost.

When he finally spoke there was anger in his voice.

"So you think that Teddy Delaney's presence at that meeting means he had something to do with Matthew Coyle's death?" he said accusingly.

I was astonished. But a moment later I almost laughed with relief. I understood now why he had been so touchy. He was protecting his friend's reputation.

"Father O'Sullivan, I don't think anything of the sort! I believe that Matty Coyle trusted Father Delaney absolutely. They were friends and allies..."

He seemed taken aback. He looked down at the table again, in confusion, and unfolded his arms. I sensed I had landed a telling blow. Father O'Sullivan was debating with himself what to divulge.

But at that crucial moment we were interrupted. The door of the bar opened and a tall, dapper figure entered. To my consternation I saw that it was another of my 'guests'. The rendezvous was not working out as I had planned.

32.

The tall, suave figure hesitated at the doorway, then stepped nonchalantly into the room and came over towards us.

"Sorry, did I interrupt something important?"

It was Councillor Joe Dougherty. Slowly he took off the leather coat he had been wearing and sat down on a chair at the next table to ours.

I had to admire his style. But just at that moment I hated his guts. He had managed to cut Father O'Sullivan off just when he was about to tell me something important. I glared at him, asking myself whether it was true what young Bob declared with such certainty—that this man had both organised and committed killings. I wasn't sure of the answer, but at that moment I wanted it to be true.

"Fancy meeting you here, Mr. McCausland!" he said. "You seem to be making a habit of coming sniffing round these parts...And this time you've chosen such suitable company! Perhaps you thought that was the best way to get in here..." He nodded to the two priests.

They seemed to know exactly who he was. Father Donnelly nodded back, with a murmured greeting.

"So have you changed the venue of your meeting?" Dougherty asked.

"No," I answered. "This was just a friendly pint before we went on there."

"Aaaah," he said knowingly. "So this is a sort of Last Supper, is it? Before we go on to the appointed place?"

I didn't like the allusion, so I tried to ignore it.

"You know that Matty Coyle and Father Delaney came here," he said nonchalantly, "on that fateful evening?"

"No," I said, trying to appear disinterested. I could see that the turn of the conversation had also disturbed Father O'Sullivan. He was shifting uneasily in his seat.

"Oh yes," Dougherty went on, "it was well known at the time. They met Al Brannigan himself, at this very table, I believe, near the window, and he gave them instructions for their 'peace meeting'..."

"Instructions?" I queried him, "or just his opinion?"

"Oh instructions. They were working for him, after all."

"Nonsense!" muttered Father O'Sullivan. He reached suddenly for his glass and knocked back what whisky remained in it. "Brannigan may have thought he owned everybody and everything. But Teddy Delaney wouldn't have just taken orders!"

Dougherty glanced at him with a hint of amusement. "Please yourself, father," he said.

He went and ordered himself a drink, without offering to buy a round for the rest of us. I thought of leaving before he came back, but felt it might be the wrong move. After all, I did want him to come to the meeting I'd arranged.

"So what *is* all this, Mr. McCausland?" Dougherty asked as he sat down, this time on our table. "The final scene of the melodrama, where Hercule Poirot unmasks the guilty party?"

I smiled. "More like a bit of experimental theatre," I replied. "Let's say that I'm trying to recreate a scene which happened over sixty years ago. And if it's successful I'm hoping it might tell us what really did happen on that occasion."

"Aaah! So it *is* the 'Last Supper', or shall we way, the 'Betrayal in the Upper Room', featuring our good friend Matty Coyle! So you think that's where Matty's last meeting with his friends, and enemies, took place? Right there at the mill, in the upper room?"

"I don't know," I said. The actual location of that fateful 'peace meeting' in 1935 had in fact been bugging me for some time. I knew it had been somewhere at the mill. But whereabouts exactly? When I thought about it, the upstairs room in the millhouse did seem as likely a place as any.

"What do *you* think?" I asked.

"No idea," he said, shrugging. "And who was it that Matty was meeting that night, now? Did I not pick up from somewhere that he was meeting…was it your father?"

I found his sarcasm hard to stomach, but I ignored it as best I could. "My father was definitely there…but so were a number of other people, I believe."

"And what makes you believe that?" Dougherty asked.

"Something that his sister Lottie told me."

He had begun to lift the beer glass to his mouth, but stopped abruptly and put it down again.

"You've been talking to Matty Coyle's sister?" He turned quickly towards me. "You mean, she's still alive?"

("You know she's alive!" I said to myself.) But I only nodded.

Suddenly he seemed angry. Obviously the news of my meeting with Lottie upset him. But he took a mouthful of his beer and some of his previous poise returned.

"So how is our re-creation of history going to work?" he asked.

"I don't know. That depends on what you and Father O'Sullivan have to tell me, along with the two other gentlemen I've asked to come."

Dougherty again raised his eyebrows, as if impressed. "And has Father O'Sullivan told you anything interesting or useful so far?"

"No, nothing much," I answered drily. "We were just getting somewhere when you interrupted."

"Oh, I'm so sorry! Please don't mind me! Go ahead…"

I would have preferred to keep all this until the whole company was united, down in the mill house. But if Father O'Sullivan had decided to throw light on anything at that moment, it would perhaps be a mistake to stop him. He was sitting gloomily looking out towards the car park and the bridge. For several moments he didn't seem to want to speak. Then he turned towards us with a determined, almost defiant look in his eyes.

"I warn you," he said, and to my surprise I noticed his voice was trembling slightly, "that what I have to say is probably not what either of you expect or want to hear."

"I don't think," I said quietly, "that anything would really surprise me much about this affair. Please just tell us what you know, Father O'Sullivan. It doesn't matter what we may or may not want to hear."

But at this moment the younger priest, Father Donnelly, chose to interrupt. He had been looking from one of us to the others, in turn, clearly aware of the tension beginning to rise around the table. And he had continuously been glancing nervously at his watch.

"Excuse me, Father O'Sullivan," he said, "but you know we have to do that one last errand…before we set off back home."

"Oh yes," said the older priest, clearly a bit put out at being interrupted. "I'm afraid we'll have to leave you for twenty minutes or so, maybe half an hour. We have one last visit to make. But with any luck we'll be able to join you again, down at the mill."

I started to protest, but Father O'Sullivan just held out his hand and said: "We'll come to the mill in twenty minutes, maybe half an hour." And with that he and his companion got up and left.

I slumped back into my seat. Dougherty and I sat there in silence for several minutes. At any moment I expected him to make some cheap joke at my expense, but finally all he said was:

"Is that the last we'll see of them, do you think?" I feared so, but didn't want to admit it. I looked at my own watch.

"Blast!" I said. "It's past the time for the rendezvous. And there were two others supposed to come…"

"Oh yes?" he said. "Like to tell me their names?"

"Why don't you come yourself and see?" I said, turning his ironic tone back on him. "We can walk down together. We've walked together down dark lanes before, haven't we? No reason to distrust one another…"

He gave me a wry smile in response. "I'll join you when I've finished my drink," he said. "You go on by yourself…"

33.

It was barely half a mile from the Inn to the mill house.

The glen, I found, had changed its face again. Gone were the warm air and droning insects of my first visit, and even the misty calm of the second, only a few days before. The wind had started to rise, and as I left the tarred road and strode down the narrow track towards the mill, the firs on either side were beginning to stir uneasily. Tufts of grass by the roadside twitched in the darkening afternoon light, and the last remaining leaves on the hazel and birch-trees rustled impatiently as a cold breeze began to funnel down the narrow confines of the valley.

As I approached the mill through the last stunted oaks I saw that the car park was still empty. That made me nervous, I don't know why. A car or two would have meant company, whoever it might be.

Unless, of course, someone had not wanted to draw attention to themselves by arriving in a car.

I cut off the lane into the trees and hung about there for several minutes, watching for any movement near the mill that might betray the presence of an uninvited guest. Someone, perhaps, who knew of our meeting but was not on my cast list. Or maybe someone who was invited, but wasn't keen to be there!

But after a few minutes of careful movement through the trees, with my eyes fixed on the building below, I was reasonably confident that there was nobody there. Nobody and nothing, nothing at all. Only the unrelenting breeze, and the stirring of the branches. They were the only signs of a living presence.

That disappointed me in another way. Perhaps my guests were not going to rise to the bait after all. Perhaps the whole enterprise would be a failure. It was beginning to look that way. But at least, I decided, it was safe to go on to the meeting place, the upper room.

As I approached the mill building I tried to avoid looking over at the tiny bridge and the mill race. In my mind's eye I could still see the flabby shape I had taken for a log, bobbing up and down in the surge of the water. And the hand. And the face. But I couldn't afford this evening to become emotional or allow my thoughts to dwell on such things. I needed a clear head and a steady hand for what I had in mind.

As I came close to the building I glanced to my left, towards the cramped car park and the copse of half-grown birches beyond it. Only then did I glimpse what looked like something metallic in the undergrowth.

Puzzled, I stopped and crossed the lower end of the car park to investigate.

Amid the long grass under the young trees was a motor-bike. It was a brightly coloured green-and-red Japanese machine lying on its side. No real attempt had been made either to park or to conceal it.

Could it belong to a hiker, I wondered, someone who had gone wandering up the lakeside path? It seemed a strange time of day to go walking in the glen. And there was something about the powerful machine that didn't fit well with the idea of a casual walker. And why, if he had just left it here while he exercised his limbs, had he half-hidden it in the long grass and bushes like this? He could easily have parked it in the car park, or by the side of the mill house.

I glanced warily round, suddenly on my guard. I ventured a little further in among the saplings, peering into the undergrowth beyond. No, I thought, you're even more vulnerable in there. I was beginning to feel really quite scared. I hurried back towards the building, past the tiny bridge. From here I had a clear view both upstream, towards the lake, and downstream, to where the little river curled sluggishly round a bend under some willows. Nothing unusual. And no sign of the bike's owner. Or of anyone else.

Where are they all? I had invited four. I knew where two of them were. Or thought I did. But where were the other two?

I reached the bottom of the wooden staircase I had explored on my last visit and began to climb the wooden stairs up the side of the building.

Suddenly I stopped. What if one of them had indeed arrived, on the motorbike? What if he had already climbed to the upper room, to wait for me? Might it not be wiser to stay out here in the open until one of the others arrived?

At that moment I heard the harsh scrunching noise of tyres in the stony lane which I had just descended. I hurried back down the stairs and round to the parking place.

It was, to my great relief, Father O'Sullivan. He and Father Donnelly were just climbing out of their beat-up old VW. The back of the vehicle was totally taken up by what looked like an enormous box.

"Just had to collect this thing," Father O'Sullivan said chirpily. "A present from Father Donnelly's family in Dungiven. We've needed a new fridge at St. Francis's for years..."

I glanced curiously at the giant shape in the rear of the car. It was draped with a blanket or tarpaulin, so it could have been anything. A curious way to carry a fridge, I thought. But was there any reason to be suspicious of the two priests? I decided not. They were probably going to be my only allies.

"Glad you came back," I said, meaning it. "Unfortunately no one else has turned up yet...Except maybe for one."

I indicated the dim outline of the motor-bike, its brightly-painted colours just visible through the undergrowth beyond the car park. "But I don't know which one. He hasn't shown himself yet."

The two priests looked at each other doubtfully, as if wondering what they had let themselves in for.

I led the way round the end of the building and began climbing the stairs to the upper room. I started to chatter aimlessly to the two priests, just to underline to anyone who might be up there that I was not alone. When I reached the glass door I took a deep breath, pushed it open and stepped in.

There was a man sitting on the far side, silhouetted against a window.

"Hello," he said. "What kept you?"

34.

"How on earth did *you* get here?" I asked.

"I came down the lane, like you did," Dougherty said scornfully. "Only I didn't bother to go skulking round the bushes first."

I was flabbergasted. I could have sworn that nobody had passed me.

"And the motor-bike?"

He shook his head. "Not mine," he said gravely.

"And you haven't seen anyone else?"

He seemed to think for a moment, then shook his head again.

I walked over to one of the windows and looked out on the grey scene below me. The wind was becoming really strong now, stirring the waters of the lake into tiny furrows. The empty boughs of the trees were swaying and shaking, and the bushes and undergrowth full of movement and agitation. Even if there had been someone hiding out there among them, it would have been difficult to pick him out.

"You were about to tell us a story, Father O'Sullivan," Dougherty said, "back there at the inn. But then you went off to give someone the last rites."

I forgot my worries about the motor-bike and turned from the window, keen to hear Father O'Sullivan take up his story. But he obviously hadn't liked Dougherty's last quip and for a moment I feared he might just stalk out of the room and leave us. I tried to give him a reassuring smile, and said:

"I'd be very grateful if you could go on from where you left off, Father O'Sullivan."

He pulled a face, but nonetheless sat down on an old packing case near a wall.

"I'll tell you all I know, but I really must be going soon."

I nodded.

***

"The meeting took place," he began, "here in this very room, at five o'clock on 24th October 1935."

He paused, and for the merest flicker of a moment I had one of those strange experiences of *deja vu* which everyone talks about but no one can adequately explain. There were four of us there, in the darkening room, and we were expecting at least one more. And I had the very definite feeling that I had been there before, in that exact same situation. The illusion was so strong that for a moment my eyes seemed to lose their focus, and Father O'Sullivan's voice appeared to be coming from a long distance away.

When my concentration returned Father O'Sullivan was some way into his story.

"...Lexie McCausland arrived first, with Matty. They had come down the glen, from the McCausland farm. Teddy Delaney was waiting at the Three Corners. Matty came up to collect him, leaving McCausland down at the mill to wait for the others. Teddy had a bicycle with him, but he didn't ride down on it. He pushed it beside him as he walked down the lane with Matty...He recalled that when they arrived at the mill your father, Mr McCausland, was standing on the parapet, looking out across the lake."

"He seems to have had a good head for detail, old Father Delaney," Dougherty commented.

Father O'Sullivan ignored him. "It was Lexie McCausland who had done all the organising. He knew who was invited and who was not. And when they were waiting for the others to arrive...I'll come on to them in a moment...your father went to great pains to explain that the other people who were coming had to be there, even if Matty and Father Delaney didn't like it. Father Delaney said that your father looked tired, and also..."

He paused.

"And also what?" I prompted him gently.

"And also very nervous."

Father O'Sullivan stopped.

"You mean," I said, "that Father Delaney had the impression my father was hiding something. Is that it?"

The priest made a non-committal gesture.

"Let's get this right," I said slowly and deliberately, anger rising within me despite myself. "Once again you're implying, that my father might have been nervous because...he had lured Matty into a trap? In other words, that he set him up. Is that it?"

"People could be forgiven for thinking that, couldn't they?" said Father O'Sullivan stiffly.

Dougherty, I noticed, for once said nothing. He had taken up a position by one of the windows, looking out over the lake the way I had done a few minutes before.

"But did Father Delaney actually say he believed that?" I asked. "That my father set a trap for Matty?" I was beginning to rebel against the idea.

The elderly priest was silent for several moments, as if considering carefully what to answer.

"No," he said finally. "In fact he underlined the fact that afterwards...your father seemed genuinely distraught, and swore he wasn't responsible for what happened. He begged Father Delaney to believe him…"

It took several seconds for the words' meaning to sink in. I sat there, and slowly a strange feeling of elation spread over me. He had gone at least part of the way to exonerate my father.

"Thank you," I said very softly. "Thank you for telling me that…"

The elderly priest looked at me sympathetically enough, and for the first time I caught a hint of sadness in his eyes. "Yet I want you to realise, Mr Mc-Causland," he said, "how it must have appeared to a lot of people."

"Yes," I murmured, "yes. I suppose it must…But it means a lot to me, what you just said. You can't imagine…"

"Yes I can," he said abruptly. "God, man, of course I can…"

I couldn't speak for several moments. Then I said:

"Father Delaney did believe my father, didn't he? And that's probably one of the reasons his story was never published. It didn't suit some people, because he was a convenient scapegoat."

Father O'Sullivan said nothing more.

For at least a minute there was silence in the room. It was interrupted by a sudden heavy thump as the glass door, which we'd left ajar, was blown back by the wind and hit the wall. Dougherty, who was closest to it, stepped across and closed it. The light was fading outside, and the small room was growing dark.

"Is there a light in here?" asked Dougherty in an irritated voice, fumbling around on the wall by the door. He seemed to be losing his composure, I noticed. It was as if the wind and the darkness were starting to unnerve him.

"We still haven't established who else came to the meeting," I said.

But Father O'Sullivan's willingness to speak seemed to have dried up. It was as if he'd suddenly come to the conclusion he was saying too much.

"So who were the others at the meeting? And what happened?" I prompted him again. "How did it come about that Matty…ended up the way he did?"

At that moment Dougherty found the switch and the room was suddenly bathed in a cold, bright light.

"That's always been quite clear," Dougherty said, his ironic tone returning. "It's always been clear what happened to Matty. He was waylaid on his way home by a gang of loyalist thugs…and they beat him up and threw him in the lake."

I looked at him coldly.

"I think it was a bit more complicated than that," I said. "I think the whole thing would become much clearer if we knew who it was actually came to the meeting. I have it from a good source…" Dougherty raised his eyebrows at this, "that there was at least one uninvited guest at the meeting, someone who shouldn't have been there. I want to know who that person was…Perhaps you, Mr Dougherty, have some ideas?"

Again he raised his eyebrows. "Me? But why should I have any notion who was there?"

"You can guess, can't you? Do you think, for instance, that Al Brannigan was there that evening? Give us the benefit of your wisdom."

Dougherty suddenly became more serious. He was eyeing me suspiciously, as if he thought I was playing some game with him. He too seemed reluctant to speculate about my questions. Perhaps he felt that the 'simple' version of events, that Matty had been betrayed by my father and killed by Protestant thugs, was in danger of unravelling. He gave a twisted smile.

"Wisdom! If it's wisdom you're after it's never been one of my strong points..."

"Was Brannigan there?"

Dougherty didn't answer at once. Then he said emphatically: "No, I'm pretty sure he wasn't. He wasn't there himself. He sent Father Delaney to represent him. They got on well, it seems. Al trusted the good father."

"So who do you think was there from the Protestant side? Apart from my father, that is?"

He looked surprised.

"You think there was somebody there from the loyalists?"

"Or just the Protestant side...The local rector, for instance, or a Presbyterian minister? As a counterpart of Father Delaney?"

Dougherty passed a hand over his chin. All of a sudden he was quite serious. "Now it's funny you should say that. For a long time I was convinced that that man McIlroy had something to do with it all."

I raised my eyebrows.

"You mean the preacher who was giving Cyril Beamish such a hard time?"

"Yes...I got this from an old man in Upperfields who was around at the time. He said McIlroy had been helping organise the gangs that went round roughing up Catholics and burning haystacks..."

"Doesn't sound like the sort of thing a minister would sanction..."

"But he wasn't really a proper minister, was he? Just a self-appointed 'representative of God' with a shrill voice and a lot of fire in his belly...But I have to admit I never got confirmation that it was him at the meeting. I think the old man thought that just because there was a gang of thugs involved...And he associated McIlroy with thugs..."

"I heard," volunteered Father Donnelly, "that there was a senior policeman involved. And that it was the B Specials who attacked and killed Matty Coyle."

I smiled condescendingly at the young priest. "Was there a name mentioned? Or any evidence to support what you heard?"

He looked unsure of himself. "I think the Sergeant in Dungiven was called Murphy. He was one of the few Catholics in the police...And I suppose that would have made him someone they would invite, because…if you see what I mean…he could see both sides of the argument."

I nodded. It was a possibility I hadn't considered.

Just then I thought I saw a shadow cross the open doorway, behind the young priest. The others must have seen it too, because we all turned in that direction. The glass-panelled door rattled in the wind, but this time did not burst open.

"Did you see something go past he door just now?" asked Dougherty hoarsely, and I noticed he reached automatically inside his jacket.

Then the shadow loomed up again, this time just outside the door. The door handle began to turn. And a moment later a tall and dapper figure stepped confidently into the room.

"Just checking everything was clear outside," it said in a clipped, authoritative voice.

It was DS Mervyn Ritchie.

"By the way…I can discount that last theory," he said. "Sergeant Murphy had nothing to do with the meeting. He was in Derry that day on police business."

35.

DS Ritchie, I remembered, had seen all the official papers.

"Yes, Sergeant Murphy was nowhere near here that day," he said emphatically. He walked past us all and peered out the second window, at the far end of the room, as if checking something outside. "Nor were any of his men."

"You seem very sure of that, Mr Ritchie," said Joe Dougherty. The two were obviously acquainted.

Ritchie gave him a cool look.

"Yes, I happen to be very well up on the case."

"And why's that?"

"For the simple reason that when our late friend Dr Ray Conlon requested access to police files on the case, I was asked to check through them. To see if there was anything...that shouldn't be revealed."

Joe Dougherty let out a whoop of pleasure. "Ah, it's all coming out now, isn't it?" he said with a chortle. "The RUC covering up its past misdemeanours!"

Ritchie ignored him. "So I've studied the case of Matty Coyle thoroughly," he said, "and I know a lot more about it, probably, than anyone else in this room."

The man certainly didn't lack self-esteem.

"Good!" I said quietly. "That's just what we need, DS Ritchie. A few facts, solid facts."

The look he turned on me was not just cool, it was icy. "And why should I divulge anything? Especially to present company!" He nodded towards Joe Dougherty and also, to my annoyance, at Father O'Sullivan.

"Perhaps," I said quietly, "because it might just help us work out who's responsible for the deaths of Ray Conlon and Tim McCloskey."

I started as a second figure appeared at the door.

"Come in, Flanagan," said Mervyn Ritchie. "Gentlemen, this is one of my assistants, DC Flanagan..."

"Flanagan?" said Joe Dougherty mockingly. "Not another Catholic who's sold himself to the Devil?"

"I'm a Methodist, actually," said DC Flanagan, smiling at Dougherty sweetly. He took up a position near the door.

Ritchie had turned to me. "What makes you think," he asked disdainfully, "that raking back over the embers of a sixty-year-old crime...if it was a crime...is going to help us with murders which happened last week? And in totally different circumstances?"

"Mm," I said doubtfully, "perhaps the circumstances haven't changed all that much. Anyway, could I just ask you one simple question, DS Ritchie?"

He didn't answer, so I asked anyway.

"If you've done a thorough study of the police files, who did the police think was responsible for Matty Coyle's death? No one was ever convicted of the crime, were they?"

He didn't answer. He was standing in the middle of the room, as if consciously seeking to be the centre of attention, with his hands clasped tightly behind his back.

"Or maybe the police didn't think it was a crime at all. Is that it? You suggested just now that it might have been...what, an accident?"

"There was no evidence of a crime. And the police, as always, based their conclusions on the evidence available. In this case there was just nothing to go on. Certainly not enough evidence to convict."

He paused.

"But?" I prompted him.

"But what I can tell you...if you're interested, that is...is who definitely was at the meeting."

I looked at him in disbelief. "You can?"

"And I'll tell you, Mr McCausland, only on one condition."

"And what's that?"

"That this never goes into writing! The problem with the Conlon man was that he was going to write a book about it all."

"You had a problem with that, with his writing a book?" Joe Dougherty challenged him.

"Of course," Ritchie eyed the councillor with disdain. "Things gain a lot more credibility when they go into print. Haven't you found that? If they're just verbal statements they can be dismissed as rumours. As gossip."

Joe Dougherty gave another snort of amusement.

"Here we can see why people always believe what they're told by the police!" he quipped. Then his eyes narrowed and fixed on the detective.

"It was you, DS Ritchie, who found Conlon's body, wasn't it? In the mill stream. You and Mr McCausland here...And you wanted to prevent Conlon from publishing his findings...So then. Might it be fair to say that this would... give you both a motive and an opportunity?"

"A motive for what? An opportunity for what?" Ritchie interrupted in irritation. "What are you trying to suggest?"

"Oh, nothing, nothing...I just thought I saw why someone might have an interest in silencing Ray Conlon, that's all."

"I give you my assurance, Mr Ritchie," I interrupted quickly, before the argument escalated, "that I am not going to write a book. I only want to know what happened that night. For my own peace of mind. And to do justice to Matty Coyle...Now, you were saying you could tell us who else was at the meeting on the night of 24th February."

Ritchie thought for a moment, than gave a twisted smile. "Yes," he said, "there was an uninvited guest, someone that apparently neither Matty Coyle nor your father, Mr McCausland, expected."

"And who was that?"

"One Dario Peccatini, Mr Aloysius Brannigan's much-vaunted 'security chief'."

36.

"Or should I say," Mervyn Ritchie corrected himself, "the leader of Brannigan's vigilantes?"

"No, you've got that wrong," Joe Dougherty broke in with heavy sarcasm, "the vigilantes were on the Protestant side!"

Ritchie again ignored him.

"And who told Peccatini about the meeting?" I asked.

"Take a guess yourself," said Ritchie. "If it wasn't your father...as almost certainly it wasn't, then who's left? It had to be either Matty Coyle himself, or...your Father Delaney."

"Father Delaney?" I felt a stab of disappointment.

"That's ridiculous," exclaimed Father O'Sullivan, coming towards us. "Teddy Delaney had no truck with this Peccatini fellow at all. He didn't like him or his sort of person. It obviously wasn't him who invited Peccatini..."

Yet the idea was troubling, Matty had trusted Father Delaney. So had my father. Yet when Peccatini arrived, they must indeed have thought he had betrayed them.

"No, it definitely wasn't Teddy Delaney," Father O'Sullivan repeated. "He was troubled by the arrival of this Peccatini fellow too. He told me so himself..."

Now it was all beginning to come out.

"So who did he think informed Peccatini?" I asked.

The priest hesitated. "He had great difficulty with that one. But then finally he came to the conclusion it could only have been one person."

"And who was that?"

"Al Brannigan himself."

"But Al Brannigan had chosen Matty and Father Delaney to represent him," I pointed out.

"Well perhaps he had second thoughts," Dougherty interjected, "and decided to send someone he could really trust!"

I turned to Ritchie.

"So what did the police think? Was it not probably Al Brannigan?"

DS Ritchie, however, was now playing hard to get. Having thrown Peccatini's name into the equation he seemed to think he had done his bit. He went back over to the window and gazed blankly out into the semi-darkness. Then he took an expensive looking silver cigarette case out of his pocket, chose one with meticulous care, as if they had all been different, and lit up. After several deep pulls he said:

"As I say, make your own guesses. I wouldn't myself discount Father Delaney...or Al Brannigan."

"It definitely was not Teddy Delaney!" Father O'Sullivan repeated angrily.

Ritchie glanced at him. "And can you prove that?"

Father O'Sullivan took several paces forward and stood facing DS Ritchie.

"I can't prove anything," he said defiantly. "But I can tell you who the final person was that came to the meeting."

Things were working out in my favour after all. Ritchie shifted on his feet but did not retreat before the onslaught.

"Be careful what you say, Father O'Sullivan," he said. "There might well be consequences."

"Consequences!" cried the priest. "You can keep your consequences! I know why you don't want me to speak out. It's because the final person at the meeting that night was none other than the great Cyril Beamish, MP!"

Joe Dougherty whistled.

"The icon of Unionism," he said, wide-eyed in mock admiration, "the man who went on to be Home Secretary, and the scourge of the Nationalists..."

"Indeed." Father O'Sullivan was still fuming with anger. "It wouldn't have looked very good, would it, if Mr Cyril Beamish, MP, was known to be mixed up in a murder investigation?"

The identity of the Fifth Man was not a total surprise, I thought. But it was a key discovery nonetheless. My mind began to work furiously. I got up and put myself physically between the policeman and the priest. And to distract them from their anger I began reasoning aloud.

"So Cyril Beamish was invited, presumably by my father, as someone influential on the Unionist side...I assume that my father thought Beamish might see the chance of a political triumph here...if he could defuse the Upperfields situation and come out looking like a peacemaker."

"That would be a fairly mean-minded interpretation of his motives," Ritchie said stiffly, "even if you were to accept that Cyril Beamish was present."

"Oh he was present all right," said Father O'Sullivan, still angry. "Teddy Delaney never told a lie in his life."

"But then Peccatini arrived," I continued, "and that, I suppose, would have broken up the whole thing. Tell me, Sergeant Ritchie, what happened after Peccatini arrived? Presumably my father did tell the police about that when he was interrogated..."

"I'll pick up the story," said Father O'Sullivan, now determined to have his say, "since DS Ritchie suddenly seems so reluctant to speak. Teddy Delaney described it in some detail in his memoirs..."

"His memoirs!" Ritchie burst out scornfully, "Half of it made up, I'll bet…"

"Peccatini," Father O'Sullivan went on, "was all smiles, it seems. Wouldn't say how he knew about the meeting. But once he arrived Teddy knew there was no point in going on with it. Of course Peccatini said he wanted peace too, but…he and Beamish immediately started arguing, accusing each other of organising violence, and so on. Father Delaney, Matty and your father tried to keep the peace, but it was hopeless.

The meeting broke up after only twenty minutes…"

37.

"The meeting broke up? Before anything was agreed?"

"Yes," said Father O'Sullivan emphatically.

I was thinking hard. "So the meeting dispersed. And what happened next? Who went where, and who did they go with?"

Father O'Sullivan shook his head. His anger was subsiding. He turned back towards the window. "The details become hazy after that," he said weakly as he sat down on the edge of the window sill.

"But please, there must have been more! We're so close to working out what happened that evening...Who left the meeting first?"

"Oh, Peccatini did...I remember Teddy was quite definite about that. And then Beamish...Your father and Matty Coyle stayed a while, discussing the situation with Father Delaney. You see, they wanted to organise a new meeting, one which wouldn't be disrupted like this one had..."

"So...did my father leave with Matty?"

"Yes, the three of them went out together, I think...But I'm not sure of exactly what happened then." Father O'Sullivan suddenly seemed very tired. His head sank slowly towards his chest.

"Lexie McCausland described everything," Mervyn Ritchie said suddenly, "in full detail."

Everyone turned expectantly towards the policeman. The door hadn't been closed properly, and again a sudden gust of wind burst it open again, making us all start. A second time Joe Dougherty went over and closed it.

"Father Delaney went back up the lane towards Upperfields," Ritchie began, "pushing his bike. Coyle and your father set off together up the glen. It was dark by then, very dark, it seems..."

He paused. I had the impression that even he was slightly overawed by the story he was about to tell.

"They started to walk together up the glen. That was the way home for both of them, you see. They would go together up past the lake, and then part company further up the glen. At that point there was a fork in the path, with two tracks climbing up out of the glen, one towards Dernafleck farm, the other towards Matty's home on the Moss-side..."

There was a sudden silence, and from the direction of the lake there came, above the noise of the wind and the tossing trees, the startled cry of some water bird.

"But they never got to that fork, did they?" I said.

"No. They were waylaid on the way."

Ritchie had now lost much of his usual brashness. He leaned against a wall and looked at the floor.

"Your father said he wasn't sure exactly how it happened. It was pitch black, you see, and the attackers came on them quite suddenly. Your father said he couldn't see who they were. But they pushed him away, and told him to get out quick, to go back home."

"So…it seems they were Prods? They'd come for Matty?"

"Yes," Ritchie acknowledged gruffly, evidently reluctant to concede the point.

"Did my father not try to…?" I was unable to complete my sentence.

"Oh he did, he struck out with his fists, he said. And he could hear the thumps and groans as Coyle exchanged blows with them too. But there were too many of them. They knocked your father up quite badly, he told the police, then two of them dragged him up the glen and left him at the bottom of the path leading up to the McCausland farm."

"And what about Matty?"

Ritchie shook his head.

"All your father could say was that he never saw Coyle again…One of your father's arms was broken, you see, so he apparently lost consciousness…And it wasn't till near the morning that he managed to crawl up to the farm."

In spite of myself, my main emotion at that moment, I acknowledge, was relief. I now knew my father had not betrayed Matty Coyle. That much was clear.

We were all silent for several minutes. None of us knew what to say.

"You know where they found him, don't you?" Ritchie asked at last.

"You mean Matty?" I shook my head.

"They found him half way between the little island that's out in the lake, half way between that and the shore. In a couple of feet of water…"

"How in heaven's name did he get there?" asked Dougherty.

"The police worked out that someone had left him on the island, and…he'd drowned trying to get back to the shore."

Another surprise. For a few moments I struggled to work out what he was saying. "So, let me get this straight. It's possible he wasn't murdered at all! He could simply have drowned while trying to make his way to safety…"

Ritchie shrugged. "That's more or less what the coroner suggested," he said.

"But…it's possible, isn't it? Even quite likely…"

The Detective Sergeant pulled a face.

"They wanted to put two Protestants on trial, you know, afterwards. The men admitted they had attacked Coyle and 'roughed him up' a little. And that they'd then taken him and put him on the island. Just to scare him, they said. But they denied any intent to kill him. And the case never went to court. The police decided there was no evidence of murder..."

"Of course they did," Joe Dougherty sneered.

"...The men weren't from the area anyway. So they were quietly shipped back to Belfast, where they came from. Your father apparently protested. But it was pointed out to him that it wouldn't be difficult to implicate him in the attack...After all, he was the only person who was definitely on the scene. And there were ways of making it look..."

He didn't complete the sentence. But I understood.

***

It's impossible to describe what I felt at that moment. A huge surge of anger welled up inside me, at what they had done to my father. They had obviously let it out that he had taken part in the attack. He was the last person to be seen with Matty, they had pointed out. And the lie had been believed, even by my father's own family.

He had wanted to build bridges, along with Matty. But in one fell swoop they had destroyed the rickety, fragile structure that the two of them had managed to put together so laboriously. One of them had been killed. The other had lived under a cloud of suspicion for the rest of his life. Suspicions which he might well try to dispel. But people would nod their heads sceptically, and exchange knowing glances...

No wonder, I thought, that my father always seemed so preoccupied when he brought us back to Banagher. I had always wondered why he rarely left the farm during our visits there. And if neighbours—Catholic or Protestant—came to visit, he would always go out for long walks, by himself.

"Well, that's that then," said Joe Dougherty grimly. The playful, mocking tone had disappeared from his voice. "Now we know who really did it. And of course, why it was covered up...Just one more miscarriage of justice."

Indeed, I thought, that was that. We had it from the horse's mouth.

But when I glanced at Ritchie he seemed preoccupied. As if he wanted to say something more. He was poking moodily with his toe at some debris on the floor.

"Is that all there is to it, Sergeant Ritchie?" I asked. "Do you think Matty Coyle just drowned?"

Ritchie didn't answer at once. But finally he pursed his lips and said:

"He had bruises all over, of course. Because despite what the two arrested men said, they had obviously given him a good going over...But there was one particular bruise...on the back of his neck, as if he had been hit a great whack with some sort of cudgel. The two men were adamant they hadn't hit him round the head. They insisted very strongly on that point..."

"Of course you all believe implicitly what a couple of Prod thugs said?" Dougherty commented drily.

Ritchie finally lost patience. He raised his finger and pointed it in Dougherty's direction. "Look, would you just shut your trap for a moment. I'm trying to say something very difficult here...And maybe very important."

"Go on, Mr Ritchie," I said to him.

He took a deep breath. "The defence lawyer hired for the two men called a medical expert who said the blow hadn't been the cause of death. Coyle did drown, you see..."

"So what's the relevance of the blow to the head?" asked Father Donnelly, who had been following every word from the far corner of the room. "If he drowned, the blow to the head isn't relevant..."

"Ah but I think Mr Ritchie is saying that it is," I interrupted. "Aren't you, Mr Ritchie?"

He neither confirmed nor denied it.

"I think what Detective Sergeant Ritchie is suggesting...correct me if I'm wrong, Mr Ritchie...is that Matty was attacked a second time. He was dumped on the island by the two men and their accomplices. He woke up some time later, and was trying to get off the island...through the shallow water and mud. That he was struck over the head with a heavy instrument. That he fell in the mud. And was drowned."

I knew from personal experience how treacherous the mud in that lake was.

The wind heaved against the door again. But again it held.

"Something like that," said Ritchie. "The defence lawyer made it sound something like that."

Father Donnelly obviously had an enquiring mind. "So what would that mean?" he asked. "That Matty Coyle was trying to get off this island, and someone didn't want him to escape? So that someone went out on a boat, and caught him when he was on his way back to the shore? With an oar, maybe. And he drowned...?"

Ritchie was staring out the window, trying not to look at any of us. "That's a possibility," he said.

As he said the words, a chill tingle of apprehension ran down my spine.

"And who could have done it?" I asked hoarsely. "The same group that attacked him in the wood? Did they come back to finish off the job and make sure he didn't escape?"

"Of course they did," said Dougherty. "That's obvious!" But even he didn't sound totally convinced.

"It's possible," said Ritchie. "It's possible…"

"But if they'd wanted to kill him, why did they take him to the island in the first place? Could somebody else, perhaps, a little later…?"

Nobody answered my question.

38.

"Who was the other person you said you'd invited?" asked Father O'Sullivan suddenly. "You said earlier there would be four of us this evening. And that didn't include Father Donnelly."

"Yes," I said, "it's strange that he hasn't turned up yet."

"Who was it?" asked Ritchie.

"Oh, someone you may well know...The editor of the Coleraine Constitution, Darius Beckton."

"Hm!" Ritchie made a dismissive noise. "Of course I know him. Very precise, pedantic sort of fellow, always correcting people's English! So I'm not the only one invited from the Protestant side! That's reassuring."

I made no comment.

"Darius!" said Dougherty disdainfully. "What sort of poncey name is that?"

"Originally Persian, I think," I said.

"Yes," said Father O'Sullivan, "but you get it in some other countries as well...When I was in Rome I knew a Father Dario Lentini, for instance. I think Dario is the same name as Darius..."

"What's wrong with you?" Joe Dougherty asked me suddenly. "You look as if you've seen a ghost."

I really was feeling a bit faint. I had just had one of those experiences when you feel you've woken up suddenly from a long sleep. I went over to open the door and stepped out on to the little platform outside, for some air. It was almost dark now, and a thin drizzle had begun to fall, slanting down through the gloom, its drops catching the light from the open doorway. It was cold and unpleasant outside, so once the fresh air had revived me, I turned and went back inside.

"No," I said, "perhaps Mr Beckton won't be coming after all."

They all looked at me curiously.

"Why do you say that?" asked Father O'Sullivan. "After all, the rest of us came, even though we..."

"No, you see I've suddenly realised something...I think it's very unlikely Mr Beckton will come."

I sat down heavily on an empty packing case. After a few moments I looked pointedly at Mervyn Ritchie.

"It's a pity you didn't tell me about Peccatini being at the meeting sooner,"

I said. "If you had we might have been able to prevent at least one murder, maybe two."

"What the devil do you mean?" he replied, clearly offended.

"Beckton. The name. He once told me it was Huguenot, Beccatin. Doesn't that, well, suggest something to you?"

"No, not particularly," he answered.

"Beccatin. Peccatini. Don't they strike you as being just a little bit similar?"

Ritchie screwed up his face. The others were also looking puzzled.

"And think also, " I went on, "about what Father O'Sullivan said about Dario being an *Italian* name..."

"You mean," Father O'Sullivan came towards me, "that this Darius Beckton may be...a Peccatini?"

Joe Dougherty stood up too. "Hey, you're letting you imagination run away with you."

"What was Peccatini's first name?" I asked Ritchie. "You mentioned it earlier, I think."

"Dario," he said. "Yes, I'm pretty sure it was Dario..."

"Darius Beckton, Dario Peccatini...It sounds suspiciously close, doesn't it?"

Joe Dougherty waved his hand dismissively. "Pure coincidence," he said.

"And Beckton is a Unionist!" Ritchie pointed out.

My certainty wavered. Yes, there was that small problem. But then I caught sight of Joe Dougherty's face.

He had suddenly stopped in the middle of the room. The dismissive, ironic smile had frozen on his face.

"Did you want to say something?" I asked him.

Dougherty turned to Ritchie. "Where did friend Beckton come from, anyway?" he asked.

Ritchie shrugged. "Turned up about ten years ago," he said, "if I remember right. I've heard him say that he's from somewhere in County Down originally. Said he'd worked in newspapers in America before 'returning home', as he put it..."

"That's interesting," I said. "He told me he was local, from County Derry. And that he'd only spent a few months in the US..."

We all stood there, saying nothing. It was Dougherty who spoke next.

"I always did think he had pretty good sources on the Republican side...for a Unionist."

Ritchie shook his head. "I still don't believe it," he said.

"Why not?" Dougherty asked.

"I would have known. I would have heard something..."

Dougherty laughed. "Your intelligence isn't as good, DS Ritchie, as you thought it was. The more I think of it, the more…Yes, I bet he was busy passing on titbits to the Republican lads all the time!" And he went on laughing.

Ritchie was looking like thunder. "You would know all about that, wouldn't you!"

"You really had no suspicions?" I asked Dougherty.

He shook his head, still chuckling to himself.

The storm outside had now reached a crescendo, buffeting the sides of the stone building and rattling the windows of the upper room. I turned to the policeman.

"If I were you, DS Ritchie," I said, "I wouldn't waste any more time. Beckton hasn't come here. But I think he may be about to leave his comfortable life in Coleraine."

"What do you mean?"

"I mean that you have a couple of unsolved murders on your hands. And I think you now may have a new suspect."

He looked annoyed. Then confused. But I persisted.

"I'd lay a bet that our friend Beckton…or maybe he's now Peccatini again… has flown the roost. I think you should be trying to stop him leaving the country."

He hesitated, but only for a moment.

"Flanagan," he said to his assistant, still standing patiently near the door, "you heard what the man said. Get on to the station in Coleraine and tell them to detain Mr Darius Beckton as soon as possible. As a matter of priority. That's Darius Beckton, one-time editor of the Coleraine Constitution. Got it?"

Flanagan disappeared at once.

"I'd better go with him," said Ritchie after a moment. "This is too important a case…" And still looking just a little flustered, he followed his assistant.

The four of us who remained stood there for a minute or two in silence.

"But why," asked Father O'Sullivan finally, "would Peccatini's son, or grandson, if that's what he is, have any interest in bumping off Ray Conlon? And poor Tim McCloskey as well?"

"He would only have an interest in it," I said, "if he thought they were coming too close to an embarrassing truth."

"Which was?"

"That old Dario, his grandfather, had had something to do with another murder. The murder of Matty Coyle."

"And…he wanted to cover the fact up," agreed Father O'Sullivan grimly.

"Might I suggest," said Joe Dougherty, who was sitting on his box again, literally twiddling his thumbs, "there may be another reason too. If Ray Conlon or anyone had made the connection between himself and Al Brannigan's pet enforcer, it might have given him some considerable embarrassment. I mean, it wouldn't have looked so good for his Unionist credentials."

"In short, it would have blown his cover?" I said.

"That's the gist of it," he agreed.

"Poor Ray Conlon," said Father O'Sullivan. "He was getting altogether too close to finding the truth about who killed Matty Coyle. But why Tim McCloskey?"

"Tim McCloskey wasn't supposed to die," I said. "The booby trap was meant for me."

39.

"Well, I'd better be going myself," said Joe Dougherty, picking up his leather jacket and hanging it over his shoulders. "The voice of the people calls...back to the grindstone."

"Just a moment, Mr Dougherty," I stopped him. "I've something else I'd like to clear up..."

He looked at me suspiciously.

"Did you ever hear the one about the Orangeman and the priest?" I asked. "No offence, fathers," I added, nodding towards the clerics on the other side of the room.

Dougherty gave an disdainful snort, but I went on anyway.

"It goes like this...The parish priest falls ill and needs an urgent blood transfusion. But the only one in the village with the same blood group is the master of the local Orange Lodge..."

"What's he blithering about?" Joe Dougherty asked, by now quite obviously annoyed. "What's this got to do...?"

"So anyway," I persisted, "they ask the Orangeman to give a few pints and, after a bit of reflection, he says: 'Och yes, I wouldn't like to see the poor man die, whatever he may be...' So they do the operation and the priest recovers. And being a Christian man he goes, with some trepidation, to thank the Orangeman. 'Ah, don't think anything of it,' says the Orangeman. 'I would have done it for any man...But there's just one thing, he says, that worries me: What's the Pope going to say when he discovers you've Orange blood flowing in your veins?'"

The three of them looked at me blankly. I completed my story.

"'Ach,' says the priest, 'to hell with the Pope!'"

There was a stony silence. Father Donnelly finally let out a little chuckle. But Joe Dougherty looked at me as if I was mad. "What are you on about?" he said. "That's one of the oldest, lamest jokes I've ever heard."

"I'm suggesting that if people have the right blood in their veins they can make some quite inspired guesses at what other people are thinking...And it's funny, I've always had the impression I know exactly what you're thinking, Mr Dougherty."

His eyes narrowed further. "I'm not sure I want to hear what you're about to say...," he began.

"Tell me, where exactly were you were born, Mr Dougherty?" I asked.

I noticed that Father O'Sullivan had dropped his eyes and fixed them somewhere around the polished toe-caps of his shoes.

"Where I was born?" said Joe Dougherty incredulously. "What business is that of yours?"

"Would it possibly have been somewhere near Westport, in Mayo?"

His eyes were angry now, and I thought he was going to utter some expletive and just walk out. But a moment later he shook himself and burst out laughing.

"Well, you seem to know it already, so why should I deny it? But why are you so interested in my origins?"

"I think maybe you know why. I just wanted to check whether I'd got the identity of your mother correct..."

He looked at me thoughtfully, then nodded. "I think you have," he said.

"So you didn't die when you were three...Who brought you back to Derry?"

"My mother did, when I was fifteen years old."

"So that's why you ended up...?"

"Speaking like a Connaught man? Yes, that's why."

"And do you see your mother very often?" I asked.

"No, not often," he said softly. "Lottie used to get upset when I went to see her...so I don't go very much now."

We stood there in awkward silence.

"So would I be correct," I asked, "in assuming that we are, in fact, half brothers?"

He raised his eyebrows in a way, I had come to realise, that was a habitual gesture. "Well now, I'd never thought of that! But...but I suppose yes, you're right, we just might be!"

Slowly he began to put on the leather jacket.

"But if you don't mind, I'd be grateful if you wouldn't spread it round too much."

"You mean, it might not go down well with some of the faithful..."

"Yeah, knowing that I'm really the bastard son of a Protestant! Wouldn't be too good. Most people would understand, I admit...Even think it a good thing. But there's always the few, isn't there?"

"Indeed," I said. "But don't worry, you can count on me. I'm not sure it would go down well in my family, either."

He gave me a wry look and was about to exit, but turned back at the door.

"By the way, you wouldn't know anything about a sum of money that appears in Lottie's account every month, would you?"

I thought for a moment, then said: "I'll try to make sure it keeps appearing."

He nodded. Then raised his hand in a farewell salute, and disappeared through the door.

***

"Could you give me a lift, Father O'Sullivan?" I asked. "Just to the end of my relatives' lane."

He looked embarrassed. "Would have been glad to, Mr McCausland. But you see, we have this fridge thing in the back seat..."

I nodded. "I understand. Never mind. I'll walk back."

The two priests and I went down to the car park. Father O'Sullivan shook my hand warmly.

"I'm glad things turned out, well, the way you wanted...I'm glad your father wasn't implicated in any way."

"You could have told me that from the beginning, Father O'Sullivan, couldn't you? You knew all along that my father was an innocent party."

His confusion increased. "I thought that you might want to blame Teddy Delaney...That's stupid, I now realise. But that was my line of thinking."

"That's all right, Father O'Sullivan," I said. "I understand. He seems to have been a decent man, your friend."

He nodded, creasing his lips into a sad smile. Then he eased himself wearily into the passenger seat, and I closed the car door behind him. Father Donnelly turned on the lights and started the engine. The battered VW drove off up the lane, leaving me alone in the dark.

40.

We had extinguished the lights when we left the upper room. It was almost completely dark. But the drizzle had stopped and now and again there were fleeting glimpses of the moon, peering out from behind the ragged, scurrying clouds.

I lingered for several minutes among the tables by the mill stream, thinking of poor Ray Conlon and how fascinated he would have been to hear the full story. Suddenly I was aware of how weary I felt and sat at one of the wooden tables, staring into the dark. All other sound was drowned by the noise of the water splashing down the mill race. I reflected on what, if anything, I had achieved. A clarification certainly, for what it was worth. The knowledge that my father had not helped send an innocent man to his grave. That was good. But I also felt sorrow for the two friends I had so recently lost. And for Matty Coyle, a man that I had never known but who somehow seemed almost a friend. I thought of his last evening, here at the mill, his last walk up through the woods with my father. His fear, his loneliness.

And I thought of my father, and of the guilt he had harboured all those years. Of the lies that had been told about him. And the truth that he was never able to express.

I also felt a lingering sense of dissatisfaction.

There had been no regret, no sign of remorse, from those who had know the truth but had hidden it. Except, at the end, from Father O'Sullivan. The others had left the upper room as convinced of their own righteousness as when they entered it. Maybe even more so.

Slowly I got up and crossed the bridge. The wind had died remarkably quickly. The surface of the lake was much calmer, and a mist was even beginning to form over the water. I refrained from looking across the lake towards the tiny island which, I now knew, had been Matty's last refuge, and I began to walk up the path that followed the shoreline.

Then I stopped abruptly. I looked back towards the copse of young birches. It was almost totally dark, but in a brief flash of moonlight I saw the glint of the brightly coloured motor-bike still lying in the undergrowth. Whoever had come on it was still here.

Preoccupied with all that had gone on in the upper room, I had forgotten all about the bike. Now the questions I had asked when I first found it came back. What was it doing there, and who was its rider?

Suddenly I felt very vulnerable.

Why had I set off on the path up by the lake?

Would it not be better to turn back and go up the gravel road towards Up-perfields? I groaned at the thought. That way it was a good three miles back to the farm. It would take me ages. And would it be any safer than the path through the glen?

I told myself to be sensible. Why should I fear the lakeside path just because it was the one that Matty and my father had taken, those sixty years ago? I was allowing myself to be ruled by some superstitious whim.

I thought I had felt he first drops of rain starting again. I shook myself. Yes, mustn't let my imagination get the better of me. Darius Beckton was far away, desperately seeking to hide, probably trying to get out of the country. And when I glanced along the darkening track ahead of me, with its canopy of trees bending over the path, there was no sign of anyone. I set off up the path at a brisk pace.

After the first corner, just out of view from the mill house, the path widened out into a glade. I was half-way across this glade when I suddenly noticed a movement in the darkness to my right.

There was a man sitting there, knees together against his chest, under a tree. I could just make out that he was wearing the heavy black leathers of a biker, complete with heavy boots. A black helmet lay on the grass beside him. His gloved hands were clasped in front of him.

He hailed me.

"Ho there, stranger! Where are you going so fast?"

The accent was unusual, and familiar. It was an English accent, with a ve-neer of local twang. I knew it at once. And when I drew closer I recognised the face too.

It was Sean Hill, the man with the long, greying hair I had first seen in the newspaper office in Derry. The man I had inadvertently followed back to Up-perfields from Coleraine. The man who had threatened Shenagh Kelly with dire things if she allowed me to meet Lottie Coyle again.

"I have a message for you," he said, "from a friend."

I stopped about five yards away from him. "Your friend or mine?" I asked.

He gave a twisted smile. "Oh, we're in a jokey frame of mind today, are we? Well, to answer your question, he's certainly a kind of friend of mine, because he's paid me a lot of money to do a job. And I'm sure he would have loved to be a friend of yours, too, only you kept annoying him..."

"Look, if Joe Dougherty wanted to send me a message, why didn't he do it in person? He had at least an hour to do it, back there in the mill house..."

"Oh, Joe Dougherty isn't the friend I was speaking of, Mr McCausland sir. Oh no...The gentleman in question is quite different from plain old Joe Dougherty. Oh no, my friend is a real gentleman...And because he couldn't make it to your little get-together, back there at the mill, he sent me to...well, sort of apologise, and give you a message."

"Beckton! So that's who you've been working for!"

"But of course. He told me that you must be a bit slow on the uptake if you thought he was actually going to grace you with his presence, here of all places...and in the company of such riff-raff. I mean, Joe Dougherty, and that snobby little shit Ritchie, and...for heaven's sake, a Catholic priest! Even two, as it turned out. You do keep strange company, Mr McCausland, not at all on the level of society Mr Beckton is used to..."

"No," I said, choosing my words carefully, "Mr Beckton...or should I give call him by his real name, Mr Peccatini, is doubtless used to mixing with the lowest of the low in New York. Or Chicago? Or maybe Baltimore."

The artificial smile disappeared from Hill's face. "Now if I were you, I would just be a little careful about the way I referred to Mr Beckton, who has after all, as I say, paid me a considerable sum of money to do a job for him..." As he spoke, he slowly and deliberately took hold of the sleek black helmet that lay beside him on the ground. Moving it to one side, he revealed a pistol with a long, thick muzzle which looked like a silencer.

Strangely, I felt no panic.

"So I'm going to be the latest body," I said, "to be found washed up in Banagher Lough. You'll really give it a very bad name. The tourist office won't be pleased with you."

But the joking phase of our encounter was clearly over. Hill was no longer smiling even a twisted smile. He took hold of the gun, and I expected him to level it at me, but instead he let it hang limply in one hand, his arms crossed over his raised knees.

"No, I don't think you're going to end up in the lake. I'm going to make very sure that if you are found, it won't be here, and it won't be for a very long time."

"So where are you going to dispose of me?" I asked. "Some abandoned bog hole up on the mountain there?"

"Do you really care?" he said, the crooked smile returning momentarily to his face.

"Oh, it would be nice to know..." I said vaguely.

"I'm sorry, I know I'm supposed to give you a last wish, but that's one request I can't fulfil...simply because I haven't decided myself where to put you!"

And he raised his eyebrows at me, shrugged, and without moving from his sitting position, raised the gun and pointed it at me.

I was surprised that I heard the shot, and that I went on hearing its echo afterwards. Should I not have been dead by now? Should I not have fallen, felt pain in my chest, in my head, wherever?

But I was still standing there, in front of him, looking down at my executioner.

Had he deliberately missed, just to play games with me, prolong the agony?

If he had, he showed no signs of repeating the shot. The barrel of the gun in his hand had fallen and was once again hanging in his hand. Then it dropped on to the ground. I saw he was no longer looking at me. His head was leaning forward, as if he had simply gone to sleep.

A small sound behind me made me turn.

"I would have thought," said Joe Dougherty, "that even somebody as otherworldly as you, Mr McCausland, would know that in these parts it's dangerous to go walking alone at night. In this glen of all places. And especially when characters like Sean Hill are about."

"You shot him!" I said, suddenly feeling weak.

"Well there's a statement of the obvious for you!" he said.

"How did you...? Did you know he was here? Why...?"

"Too many questions! Let's just say that he was a bit careless, wasn't he, leaving that motor-bike where everyone could see it!"

I went and sat down, gingerly, on the remains of a fallen tree. "I expect it was a sort of bravado thing," I said weakly. "Let the victim know he's in danger. Something like that...He liked to play with his victims, didn't he?"

"Some people get like that," said Joe Dougherty, "when they get hooked on violence."

"What are you going to do with him?" I asked.

"Don't worry. I've a couple of lads on hand who will deal with him." At that moment I heard a couple of car doors banging back near the mill. "We'll take him well away from here, so nobody's going to suspect you were involved."

I looked at him, with genuine gratitude. "Why are you doing this?" I asked. "Why are you helping me?"

He had gone over to Hill's body and begun to search through the pockets of his leather jacket. He looked up.

"But we have a lot in common, Mr McCausland, don't we?"

I was baffled. "Do we?" I asked.

He bent down over the body again. "Well, it was you who told me so. You said we may have a father in common..."

He straightened up and looked over at me. "Now," he said, "I think you'd better go, before the lads arrive. The fewer people know you've been here the better. For my lads, Hill has to appear as a traitor, executed because he was really working for the Brits."

"And was he?"

Joe Dougherty shrugged. "I don't know," he said lightly.

I got up, still feeling weak in the knees, and nodded. I started to set off along the track, then stopped.

"Thanks," I called back.

He was leaning over the body again. He merely grunted.

41.

"This is a letter I should have sent some time ago," read the letter with the Mayo postmark. *"May God forgive me, but I hope you understand that there was a real conflict of conscience here. . .*

For years my old friend Father Teddy Delaney was planning to give a full account of the events leading up to Matty Coyle's death, as he knew them. And he did more or less complete them. But when it came to the crunch there were forces at play which thought the matter best left untouched. One way or another they prevented Teddy from telling his story. . .Oh I won't say exactly who they were. Certainly his bishop did not play a very positive role. He was afraid Teddy's account might bring discredit to the church. But there was political pressure on him too. . .

You see, my friend Teddy Delaney knew the affair was much more complicated than the popular version: that is, that Matty was killed by the Protestants because they wanted to close Brannigan's mill. Oh yes, the loyalists definitely had a hand in it. But if Teddy's version had got out, questions would have been asked about some people on the Catholic side too. . .

The Protestants attacked Matty and left him on the island. That much was certain. But did they do it, as the two arrested men claimed, as 'a bit of a lark'? Or did they know what was going to follow? Did they know he was never meant to get off the island? Teddy was a charitable soul, and thought it quite possible they did not. Myself, I'm much less inclined to give them the benefit of the doubt. I think the loyalists, or at least some of them, knew there was a much darker plot afoot, and that the writing was on the wall for poor Matty. Though of course I can't prove that. . .

Who actually planned the whole thing? Teddy and I discussed this over and over, and we came to the conclusion that there was only one answer. Beamish and Peccatini were in it together. They had always got along well. Who had invited Peccatini to the meeting if it wasn't Beamish? Neither Teddy nor Matty nor your father had any interest in including him in their discussions. And Al Brannigan, Teddy was sure, trusted him to do all the necessary. He wouldn't have sent Peccatini as well. . .

And Peccatini's arrival at the meeting achieved two things that both Beamish and he wanted. First of all, it allowed them to break up the meeting by arguing over basics. And secondly it allowed Peccatini, and Beamish, to keep tabs on Matty's movements that evening. They had Matty, all the time, at their mercy.

And when you think of it, Matty's death was just too convenient for both of them. Peccatini and Beamish both wanted rid of him, that's obvious. Teddy told me that Matty had really got up Peccatini's nose with his insistence that everything be done according to the book. Even though it pains me to say it, the Unionist press were right. Peccatini, for all his charm and good humour, was basically just a hoodlum. . .He wanted to hit hard at the loyalists, start burning hayricks and even buildings, in order to put the pressure on the Unionist side and force them to stop their own attacks. And Matty was against it. He knew it would just fan the flames of bitterness and hatred. Neither Teddy nor

Matty was at all convinced that moderation would succeed, with opponents like Cyril Beamish pitted against them. But they thought it was the only honourable road to follow. . .

And Beamish too wanted shot of Matty. You see, Matty was that embarrassing thing, an honourable Nationalist. And that didn't fit into his scenario at all. All the Nationalists had to be crooks, gangsters, good-for-nothings intent on mayhem and violence. Matty had also said some things, in public, which were not very complimentary about Mr Beamish. And they had hurt his dignity.

The final straw was the Ballymully parade. That made Peccatini furious, because he had planned the ambush so meticulously. And it also humiliated Beamish, when his own people refused to march with him through the village. Basically, Matty was hated by both men.

I also think, ironically, that each of them intended all along to double-cross the other. Beamish, who was clearly never short of self-confidence, was convinced he could pin the blame for Matty's killing on Al Brannigan and his American 'hoodlums'. And in a way he was right. The Unionist authorities certainly used it as an excuse to discredit the Brannigan project and have Peccatini and his men deported.

And Peccatini was equally sure he could put the blame for Matty's death on the Unionists. Matty was, after all, a Catholic campaigning for Catholic rights. who got in the way of the Unionists. . .And by and large that's the way it looked in the end. The Unionists may have managed to a large degree to hush the whole thing up and keep Beamish's name out of the news. But those who do remember the Brannigan affair mostly see it as a straight case of a murder, the murder of a Catholic by the Protestants. . .

Did Aloysius Brannigan know about the plot to get rid of Matty? At the time, apparently, many thought he did—especially those on the Unionist side. The suggestion was that Peccatini and his men had played the role of the knights who murdered Thomas a Becket in the cathedral. A 'Rid me of this turbulent priest' sort of scenario. . .But I personally doubt it. After Matty's death, Teddy told me, Brannigan seemed genuinely shocked. He cancelled the whole project and went back to America. And they say he died only a few years later, bankrupt and a drunkard.

Two final questions.

Firstly, was Matty's killing definitely planned in advance? Or could it just have been an accident? Perhaps after all the coroner was right. Might it just have been the case that Matty got stuck in the mud while trying to escape the island and drowned by accident?

You're free to believe what you like on this. But Teddy and I were both convinced that it was murder, and that whoever actually committed the murder, Beamish and Peccatini both took part in planning it. . .It was just, I suppose, our gut feeling.

So who, in the final analysis, actually did the killing? Was it the loyalists who returned and finished off what they had started, on orders from Beamish? Maybe, but of course it could equally well have been Peccatini and his men. Knowing that the loyalists would probably be blamed, and seeing that Matty was making a good fist of escaping from the island through the mud and shallow water, they may well have gone out there in a boat, hit him with an oar. . .and left him to drown.

As I say, you can come to your own conclusions. . .The one thing that's sure is that nobody really comes out of this matter with much credit. . .

Except, that is, for the honourable few we know about. . .

THE TRAGIC FATE OF MATTY COYLE

I was reading the Old Testament the other day. . .not, alas, something I do very often. . .and chanced on the book of Daniel and the story of the three men thrown into the fiery furnace: Shadrach, Meshach and Abednego. They were thrown in the fire, but the fire didn't consume them. Instead it consumed their tormentors. And there appeared beside them in the flames a radiant figure, which the king took to be an angel of the Lord. . .I thought then of Teddy Delaney, and Matty. . .and yes, of course, I have to add your father. Yes, the three of them, they were Shadrach, Meshach and Abednego. . ."

42.

"Have you found Beckton yet?" I asked Ritchie when he phoned.

"No," he said curtly. "But we will...And we've established exactly who he is."

"Oh yes?"

"He's a Peccatini all right. Dario Alessandro Peccatini...a great nephew of Al Brannigan's sidekick..."

"Great nephew?" I was astonished. "So he did all this for someone whom he can have hardly known!"

Ritchie was silent for a moment. "No," he said finally. "He had other motives, it seems."

"Really?"

"Dario had a record...In fact he was very much a wanted man in his homeland."

"In the States?"

"Yes...wanted for organising a hit on a business associate's wife."

"That's 'business associate' as in...?"

"Whatever."

"Nasty man. So he didn't come here on a mission. He was hiding, basically."

"That's it. He made a new life, with a different profession and a different life history. Who would have suspected the nice middle-class Protestant journalist of being, well, whatever he was...?"

"And that's why he was so scared of having his cover blown when Ray Conlon and I started snooping round..."

"Yes, you were a real danger to him. Or so he thought."

"But he could have been worried about family honour as well?"

Ritchie sniffed. "Maybe...By the way, the real reason I phoned...You haven't been anywhere near Greysteel recently, have you?"

"No," I said, suddenly on my guard again. "I've been taking the Claudy road when I go into Derry. Why?"

"Because we found another dead body there last night. Somebody we think you may have known..."

"Really! Who was it?"

There was a sharp intake of breath at the other end of the line. "A man called Sean Hill. Known to have been frequenting the Three Corners Inn at

Upperfields recently…You didn't happen to meet him there in the last few days, did you?"

"Only once been into the Three Corners Inn, sorry. And that was when Father O'Sullivan invited me in. Otherwise I've just driven past it…Wouldn't dare go in. From what I hear it's a pretty scary place nowadays…full of republicans…not my scene at all."

Another intake of breath.

"But did you know him?"

"Hill? No, I can honestly say I didn't know him…though he did more or less break into Lottie Coyle's house in Derry when I was there. And issue some rather nasty threats against her and the woman who looks after her…"

"In other words you did meet him."

"No, not exactly. You see Tim McCloskey and I were hiding in the back room when all this happened."

This time Mervyn Ritchie burst out in a guffaw. It was the one and only time I heard him laugh.

"There's a moral in that somewhere," he said after he'd had his chuckle.

I didn't know quite what he was implying, so I just said goodbye and rang off.

43.

I returned to see Lottie one last time.

This time I drove myself through the Bogside, and parked down the street from the house. But even as I got out of the car I saw that something was wrong. Small knots of people had gathered in the street on either side of Shenagh Kelly's house and stood in silence or in quiet conversation nearby.

I hesitated, but then came on. At first I feared that Lottie, or perhaps Shenagh, had been the victim of some appalling attack.

But then I spotted Shenagh among one of the little groups of people. She saw me too, and came over.

"Poor Lottie passed away early this morning," she said before I had time to ask.

We stood side by side for a few moments, united in a moment of sadness, no, of grief. "She's at peace now," said Shenagh quietly, looking down at the pavement. I found that no words would come to my mouth. I just did not know what to say.

"Wait there a moment," Shenagh said suddenly, and disappeared into the house. A minute or two later she came out again carrying a plastic supermarket bag, which she handed to me.

"She asked me to give you these," she said. "Just a few hours before she went."

I looked into the bag and saw a small bundle of blue envelopes, carefully tied with a piece of red string.

"They're…"

"Yes," I interrupted, "I can guess what they are."

She invited me in one last time to see Lottie, but I declined.

***

I never read the letters. They were no concern of mine. These were things that went between my father and Lottie. But I still keep them here in a drawer of my desk, unread, lying on top of three plain exercise books with orange and mauve covers.

END

Made in the USA
Columbia, SC
21 October 2023

24672390R00107